If anyone thought he was going to let them get to this woman, they'd badly overestimated their power.

"You're not alone like those other women. You're not going to be alone."

"I live alone. I walk to work and back every day, alone—"

"No more of that. You drive everywhere. No more walking alone." Gabe crossed to where she leaned against the truck, putting his hand on her shoulder. "And no living alone, either. I know you've got neighbors all around you, but that note proves the killers think they can get to you regardless. So you're not living alone, either."

"So, what—I get myself a roommate and now she's in danger, too?" Alicia shook her head firmly. "I'm not putting another woman in danger."

"Not a woman." Gabe leaned toward her. "Me."

PAULA GRAVES

THE MAN FROM GOSSAMER RIDGE

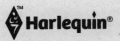
Harlequin®

TORONTO NEW YORK LONDON
AMSTERDAM PARIS SYDNEY HAMBURG
STOCKHOLM ATHENS TOKYO MILAN MADRID
PRAGUE WARSAW BUDAPEST AUCKLAND

For my sister Patty, whose indomitable spirit
can both drive me crazy and inspire me.

ISBN-13: 978-0-373-69545-4

THE MAN FROM GOSSAMER RIDGE

Copyright © 2011 by Paula Graves

Recycling programs
for this product may
not exist in your area.

www.eHarlequin.com

Printed in U.S.A.

ABOUT THE AUTHOR

Alabama native Paula Graves wrote her first book, a mystery starring herself and her neighborhood friends, at the age of six. A voracious reader, Paula loves books that pair tantalizing mystery with compelling romance. When she's not reading or writing, she works as a creative director for a Birmingham advertising agency and spends time with her family and friends. She is a member of Southern Magic Romance Writers, Heart of Dixie Romance Writers and Romance Writers of America.

Paula invites readers to visit her website, www.paulagraves.com.

Books by Paula Graves

CAST OF CHARACTERS

Alicia Solano—Her doctoral dissertation project has turned into a serious investigation of a serial-killer pair she believes has been killing women across at least three states. Could they be behind the cold case murder of the mother of one of her students?

Gabe Cooper—Torn by guilt about a mistake he believes led to his sister-in-law Brenda's murder twelve years ago, Gabe can't say no when his niece asks for his help in solving two new murders.

Cissy Cooper—Left motherless as a child by a brutal murder, Cissy believes her professor's theory about a serial-killer pair may explain all the discrepancies in her mother's murder case.

J. D. Cooper—A widower still mourning his murdered wife twelve years after her death, he's determined to bring his daughter Cissy home to safety when he learns about the coed murders in the college town where she's living.

Marlon Dyson—Alicia's fellow college instructor seems a little too interested in her new friendship with Gabe. Is he jealous? Or does he have darker intentions?

Tony Evans—The handsome policeman is Alicia's ex-boyfriend. But Gabe wonders if ulterior motives drive Tony's newfound interest in Alicia's investigation.

Tyler Landon—Alicia's student shows sudden, inappropriate interest in her just as she begins to receive threats from a stalker. Is he just a student with a crush or could he be a killer?

Prologue

Brenda was going to kill him.

Well, probably not Brenda, Gabe Cooper amended mentally. His sister-in-law was a real sweetheart who could forgive just about anything. But if she let it slip to J.D. that Gabe had shown up twenty minutes late to check on her at work, there'd be hell to pay. Gabe's older brother definitely wasn't a sweetheart and he'd have no trouble riding Gabe's back about it for ages to come.

But was it Gabe's fault that tonight was the first time his friend Cam Shelton had been home from college in almost four years? They were both over twenty-one now, and the closest place to buy a beer and shoot a little pool was a whole county over. He'd lost track of time, catching up with his old friend's rowdy tales of fraternity parties and football games in Austin, Texas. It had been after eleven before Gabe had even thought to check the time.

As he rounded a curve in the highway, he came upon a car with its bright lights on. The other car dimmed its headlights, but the afterimage of the bright orbs lingered long enough that Gabe nearly missed his turnoff. He whipped the Jeep left onto Piedmont Road, which dead-ended at the parking lot of Belmont Trucking. Taking the curve into the parking lot too fast, he swept the front of his Jeep precariously close to the large white Belmont Trucking Company sign. Righting the Wrangler, he whipped into the slot beside Brenda's silver Pontiac Grand Prix just as the dashboard clock flipped from 11:22 p.m. to 11:23 p.m.

Since the Pontiac was still here, she must have been right about the battery. She'd called him earlier that evening to ask if he could swing by the trucking company around eleven when her flex shift ended, in case she needed a jump. J.D. was out of town on Navy temporary duty, so it fell to one of the other Cooper brothers to come through for her. Gabe had been the first she'd been able to get on the phone.

He hurried up the walkway to the trucking company's entrance, a thick, steel-reinforced door set into the side of the building. Up close, he could see that the corrugated metal siding was in dire need of a good soaking rain to wash away some of the grime. The door was locked, as it generally was after five o'clock. Brenda would have to buzz him in. He rang the doorbell and waited for Brenda to answer, stamping his feet against the November cold. When she didn't answer after a minute, he rang the doorbell again.

Two minutes and several doorbell rings later, he began to worry. Flipping open his cell phone, he dialed Brenda's number. After a moment, he heard the low burr of her cell phone ringing.

Behind him.

The beer he'd drunk a half hour earlier rumbled in his gut as he retraced his steps to the Pontiac. He followed the ringing noise around to the driver's side, spotting the phone on the pavement just beneath the car door.

With his heart pounding like a bass drum in his ears, he took a couple of steps toward the ringing phone and stopped, his gaze stopping with horror on a dark streak marring the Pontiac's driver's side door. In the cold blue moonlight, it looked as black and shiny as pitch.

He swallowed the dread snaking up his throat, snagging his keys from his pocket. He turned on the small penlight attached to the key ring and played the narrow beam against the Pontiac's driver's door. In the small circle of light, the streak on the door glimmered deep crimson.

"Brenda?" He backed away from the Pontiac, his mind recoiling from what he was seeing. Maybe she'd cut herself trying to get the battery to work and she'd—

She'd what? Left her cell phone lying by the car, ignored the shelter of the building behind her and started walking the six miles to town to seek help?

He pushed down his rising panic and hurried to the Jeep for the heavy-duty flashlight he kept in a toolbox in the back. Shining the powerful beam on the scrubby bushes edging the trucking company property, he kept calling her name, hoping she'd simply become disoriented and wandered into the thick woods beyond the property.

He found her five minutes later, only twenty yards away from the parking lot, her limp body positioned between the rough trunk of a pine tree and the prickly green leaves of a wild holly bush. Her eyes were half-open, staring sightlessly at the three-quarter moon peeking through the winterbare trees. Blood stained the front of her blouse in several places.

Stab wounds.

Gabe bent to check for a pulse, tears spilling down his cheeks in icy streams. But he knew the truth before his fingers found the still place where her pulse should have been.

She was dead.

And it was his fault.

Chapter One

Alicia Solano looked up from the file contents spread across the table in front of her and gave a small start at the sight of her own reflection in the psychology lab windows. Inky twilight had fallen outside the building while she'd been working, catching her unaware.

Her pulse notching upwards, she gathered her papers into a neat stack, forcing herself to move with deliberation rather than speed. If she took her time now, her files would be in order the next time she opened her briefcase and then she wouldn't have to spend time she didn't have trying to remember where she left off.

And moving faster wouldn't make it any easier to step out into the darkness that loomed between her and the safety of her apartment.

Snapping the briefcase closed, she paused for a second in the stillness of the empty lab and listened carefully for sounds of other people remaining in the building. There would be few here this time of night; at a school as small as Mill Valley University, night classes were rare and usually limited to the business school or the continuing education classes that convened in the liberal arts building across campus.

As she headed for the exits, the faint sound of a cleaning crew chatting in rapid-fire Spanish floated from somewhere down the hall, easing her sense of isolation. Alicia relaxed, at least until she reached the heavy double doors of the exit. Once she stepped into the mild evening air, tension crept back into her spine.

It's not the right set-up, she reminded herself, images from her files flashing through her head. She was still within earshot of students moving about the quad a hundred yards away. There was also the cleaning crew in the building she'd just exited who could come quickly if she cried out. The other women had been utterly alone, in secluded places where nobody could hear their final screams.

She gripped the handle of her briefcase more tightly, grateful for its solid heft. It would make a good weapon if she needed one.

Her apartment was within walking distance of the campus, though secluded, tree-lined Dogwood Street was narrow and tunnel-like, an attribute she enjoyed during daylight hours but regretted now as she navigated the deep shadows inking the sidewalk between her and the relative safety of her apartment.

The four-unit apartment building came into view, a two-story structure rising up in the gloom like the phantom of an old Southern mansion, complete with tall white columns supporting a white-railed porch on the bottom floor and matching balconies on the second floor. The muddy golden glow of the streetlamp on the corner didn't penetrate the canopy of hickory, oak and pecan trees towering over the building, though somehow the ivory columns seemed to glow in the dark like moon-bleached bones.

Alicia quickened her pace at the corner, her low heels clicking loudly on the sidewalk. She had almost reached the steps to the apartments when she realized her footsteps were not alone. Her steps faltered, but the footfalls behind her kept coming, the pace even and unhurried.

She slipped her hand into the pocket of her light cotton jacket and closed her fingers around the small canister of pepper spray. Taking a deep breath, she turned to face her unknown companion.

He was little more than a silhouette in the cool purple shadows behind her, backlit by the shaft of streetlamp glow several yards beyond. Definitely male. Built well. Short hair, powerful shoulders, narrow waist, long legs.

Alicia's heart hammered against her rib cage, but she squelched the urge to run up the steps to her apartment. She knew she'd never make it before he caught up with her, and she'd lose whatever advantage she had gained by facing him head-on.

"Can I help you?" she asked, hating the quiver in her voice.

"I'm looking for Bellewood Manor." His voice was deep, friendly and deliciously Southern. A California girl, born and bred, Alicia had discovered a soft spot for a deep, slow drawl. She fought against letting her guard down, however. A sexy Southern accent didn't preclude very bad intentions.

"May I ask why?" she countered warily.

"My niece asked me to meet her here. Cissy Cooper—do you know her? She's a student at Mill Valley University—"

Alicia dropped her guard a notch. Cissy Cooper was one of the students in the second-year criminology lab she taught. She lived two doors down from Alicia. "I've met her."

He stepped toward her. Her heart rate edged upwards again. "My name is Gabe Cooper. I'm sorry if I scared you."

She lifted her chin. "You didn't."

"She wasn't sure she'd be here when I arrived—her shift

at the library ended at seven, but she said she sometimes has to stay late." He cocked his head, gazing up at the apartments. "Do you know which apartment is hers?"

Alicia's tension rose again. "She told you to meet her but didn't give you the address?"

"My cell signal was bad when she called."

Alicia edged backwards, suspicion eclipsing attraction at the moment. "Perhaps you should try calling her again."

"Don't you live here? I mean, you looked as if you were heading right here." He waved his hand at the building.

A car rounded the corner and started coming up the street behind Alicia, headlights briefly illuminating the stranger. He had hair as dark as her own and clear blue eyes that met hers without any shiftiness. He was trim and tall, dressed in snug-fitting jeans and a heather gray polo shirt worn untucked. The car passed, plunging them back into darkness.

"I have to go," she said, turning away from him. She'd circle the block and come back from another direction, see if the stranger had moved along or if he was still lurking there. Or maybe she'd go back and find a campus security officer to walk her safely to her doorstep.

"Is this about the murders?"

His soft query halted her steps. She turned to look at him. "The murders?"

"Cissy said something about some murders. She wanted to tell me about them. It was all very cryptic."

Alicia eyed him warily. Cissy knew about Alicia's theories, of course. The last time they'd spoken, Cissy had mentioned she was debating telling her father about Alicia's research. But she hadn't mentioned anything about an uncle.

"So you came all the way here to Millbridge because your niece cryptically mentioned murders?"

"Cissy calls and asks for my help, I come," he said simply.

"Nice uncle," she murmured. She wasn't even sure her parents would come if she called, much less any of her uncles from either side of the family tree.

"Look, I've clearly spooked you. And I guess if there are murders going on here that Cissy thinks I need to know about, you've got good reason to be a little freaked."

"I told you, you didn't scare me."

"I'm afraid I don't believe you," he answered in a slow, devastating drawl. He reached into the back pocket of his jeans. As he did so, the side hem of his shirt lifted to reveal a handgun tucked into a slim holster attached to the waistband of his jeans.

Alicia's heart skipped a beat. She pulled the pepper spray canister from her jacket pocket, ready to press the button and run like hell at the slightest provocation.

But the man who called himself Gabe Cooper merely brought out a thin, dark-colored wallet. He flipped it open with one hand and flashed a small penlight onto the contents. Alicia saw a photo ID inside.

"This is me," he said, moving closer.

She settled her trembling finger over the button of the pepper spray dispenser, but stood her ground as he came close enough for her to see the ID. It was an Alabama driver's license, with a Gossamer Ridge address. The photo of the man was impossibly good for a driver's license photo, making Alicia hate him a little in envy.

The name on the license was definitely Gabe Cooper, and she knew her friend Cissy was from Gossamer Ridge.

"Would a second ID help? I have a lifetime Alabama fishing license—"

Her tension eased again. "What do you do for a living?"

He hesitated a second, as if realizing this was a test. "I'm a fishing guide and sometimes professional angler. I also pull volunteer shifts as an auxiliary deputy at the Chickasaw County Sheriff's Department."

"What's Cissy's father's name?"

"J.D.," he answered patiently. "James Dennison, actually, but we've always called him J.D."

"What about her mother?"

He hesitated again, this time answering in a faint, emotion-tinged voice. "Brenda Alice Teague Cooper. She died twelve years ago."

"How'd she die?"

"She was murdered."

Pain etched every word into the darkness between them, reminding her of the way Cissy spoke of her mother, in a voice raw with sadness. Only with this man, the pain was rawer still, edged with a bitterness that made Alicia's stomach ache.

This man couldn't take a person's life with the impersonal ease of a serial killer. Alicia put the pepper spray back into the pocket of her jacket. "I'm Alicia Solano."

"So you're Professor Solano?" He sounded surprised. Alicia guessed his niece had mentioned her to him at some point.

"Instructor, actually. No Ph.D yet." She tried not to bristle at his skepticism. It wasn't an insult to be thought too young to be a college instructor, or so her older colleagues insisted. She was a young-looking twenty-five, especially when she eschewed makeup, as she'd done today.

"Cissy speaks well of you."

"She's a good student," she answered automatically, then softened her voice. "Good person, actually."

The shadows of his face split to reveal a flash of white teeth that even the gloom couldn't conceal. "We're kind of fond of her our own selves."

"Cissy shares Apartment D with a couple of other Mill Valley underclassmen." Alicia waved at the apartment on the far left. There were no lights burning inside on either floor of the two-story apartment. They were nearing the end of the spring semester, so any of the girls might still be at the library studying for end of term exams.

"Looks like no one's home," Gabe murmured.

"You can wait for her at my place."

He looked surprised. "You don't even know me."

She was a little surprised herself, remembering the holstered gun she'd spotted. But she was convinced he really was Cissy's uncle and he'd said he was a volunteer deputy sheriff. If Cissy had asked him to visit, he must be a pretty good guy, packing heat or not.

Besides, she had a million questions for him. Cissy had been seven when her mother died, and from what she had told Alicia, she'd been sheltered from a lot of details of the murder. What little she did know, she'd gleaned mostly from snippets of her father's conversations she'd overheard over the years and from a series of newspaper articles she'd looked up at the local library when she was in high school.

But Gabe Cooper was old enough to know everything that happened. He could answer some of the questions she had about Brenda Cooper's murder. And maybe, if she asked the right questions, he could help her catch a couple of killers.

THE OUTSIDE OF THE apartment may have been all shabby Southern charm, but inside, a riot of color greeted Gabe Cooper, nearly scorching his retinas. Pale yellow walls were the extent of subtlety inside Alicia Solano's apartment, providing a neutral backdrop for a variety of bright furnishings, from Caribbean dancers writhing in frenetic joy across a wide canvas hanging over a bright orange sofa to the lime green area rug covering the hardwood floor underfoot. It reminded Gabe of an outdoor market he'd visited in South America the last time he'd gone fishing down there, all vivid colors and kinetic energy.

"I don't drink coffee," Alicia said over her shoulder, moving out of the living room into the smaller, open kitchen area, "but I have iced tea. Or I could make some lemonade—"

He could tell by her accent that she wasn't from anywhere near the sleepy college town of Millbridge, Alabama, but she'd apparently picked up the local customs of hospitality somewhere along the way.

"Or maybe you're hungry?" she added. "Had dinner yet?"

He laughed softly. Yes, she'd learned the Southern way very well. "I'll wait and have something with Cissy when she gets home," he answered.

She paused in the middle of the kitchen, turning to look at him. "Oh, okay. Sure you don't want something to drink?"

"Ice water would be great," he answered, mostly so he wouldn't disappoint her.

She turned toward the cabinets, standing on tiptoe to reach the glasses on the top shelf. She seemed relieved to have something to do with all the bottled up energy radiating from her compact body.

He'd scared her earlier, despite her protestations to the contrary. He should have identified himself first, put her at ease. He sometimes forgot, having grown up in a little town where everyone knew everyone else, that the world could be a very different place for other people.

Brenda's murder should have etched that life lesson into his soul a long time ago.

She came into the living room bearing a glass of water and ice, a paper napkin under the bottom as a makeshift coaster. She waved for him to sit on the sofa and dropped onto a bright green ottoman nearby.

"I'm not keeping you from anything, I hope." He eyed the neon blue briefcase she'd set on the coffee table when they entered.

She followed his gaze. "Just brought some notes home to work on my thesis."

He took a sip of the water. She didn't put a lot of ice in, which meant wherever that accent had come from, it probably wasn't somewhere particularly hot. "Where are you from? Originally, I mean."

"San Francisco."

"Pretty area."

"Yes."

She watched him with a narrowed gaze, her mind working visibly behind a pair of dark, observant eyes. She didn't have any makeup on, though with her thick black eyelashes and honey-toned skin, she didn't need much. It had been hard to tell at first glance what sort of body lay beneath the loose-cut gray blouse and plain black skirt she wore. But watching her move, as he'd done when she went to the kitchen for his water, he'd quickly seen the graceful curves of her hips and spine, the straining of her round breasts against the front of the blouse when she'd risen to reach the glasses.

Surrounded by the riot of color in her apartment, she seemed almost unnaturally still in contrast, a little sparrow sitting quiet and watchful in the midst of chaos.

A shrill sound emanated from inside the blue briefcase, making her jump. "That might be a student—I have to get that." She snapped open the case and retrieved a small silver phone. She flipped it open. "Hello?"

As she moved toward the kitchen, Gabe glanced at the contents of the open briefcase. A stack of files and papers lay within, nondescript at first glance. But the edge of a photo peeked out of one folder. The only thing he could make out were a patch of tall grass and a woman's single shoe.

But it was enough to make his blood run cold.

He glanced up at Alicia. She'd moved all the way into the kitchen, her back to him as she spoke in low tones on the phone.

Gabe reached into the case and pulled out the file containing the photo. He took the photo out and stared at it, his pulse hammering in his head.

Brenda.

She lay as he'd found her, wedged between the tree and the bush, her skirt demurely in place, her legs slightly bent. Her brown pumps were still on her feet, though the police had informed the family that there had been scrapes on the heels of her feet and shredding of her stockings consistent with being dragged through the rough parking lot outside the trucking company.

When Victor Logan raped and killed her, he'd made sure she was left in a dignified position in death. Apparently he'd fancied himself a gentleman. Gabe's lip curled with disgust.

"I should have closed the briefcase."

Gabe looked up at Alicia's words. He hadn't heard her approach. "What are you doing with this?"

The look on her face was equal parts guilt and determination. "Well, I'd hoped that Cissy would get here before the subject came up, but I'm pretty sure that's why she called you to come here."

Connections started forming in his mind, though they made no sense. Brenda's murder had been solved finally, after twelve years, when his twin brother Jake and Jake's wife Mariah had put the pieces together that implicated an itinerant mechanic named Victor Logan in Brenda's murder as well as several other murders in a three-state area. Logan had died in a gas explosion at his home in Buckley, Mississippi, not a month earlier.

Cissy knew Victor Logan had been living in Chickasaw County at the time of her mother's murder and that he'd kept a scrapbook on the series of murders that had included articles about Brenda's death as well. She knew why the police believed Logan was her mother's killer, so why would she have called him all the way here just to dredge up a closed case?

"Brenda's murder investigation is over," he said aloud, dropping the file onto the coffee table dismissively. "The killer is dead."

A knock on the door sent a jolt through his nervous system.

Alicia gave a small start, too. She crossed to the front door and glanced through the peephole. Her tense posture eased and she opened the door to reveal Gabe's niece Cissy.

Cissy's green eyes met Gabe's, first with delight then with a growing sense of dismay as she sensed the tension in the room. "Has something happened?" she asked Alicia.

"He saw the file," Alicia answered quietly, closing the door behind her.

Cissy pressed her lips into a narrow line. "I wanted to set it up better, but I guess you know why you're here now."

Gabe shook his head. "Not really. How about you start telling me why you really dragged me down here?"

Cissy took his hand for a moment, then wrapped her

slender arms around him and gave him a tight, fierce hug. "I know you wanted this to all be over. I did, too." She stepped back, pinning him with the full force of her green-eyed gaze. "But it's not. Victor Logan didn't kill my mom."

Chapter Two

Alicia watched Gabe Cooper's expression go from puzzled to furious in the span of a second. His gaze whipped up to snare her own, snapping with anger so intense her stomach knotted.

"Did you put this idea in her head?" he asked.

Cissy tugged at his arm. "Alicia can't make me believe something if I don't think it's true. I'm the one who raised the subject with her, not the other way around."

Gabe turned to his niece, his brow furrowing. "Why? You heard everything Mariah and Jake told us about Logan. You know about the scrapbook—"

"Nobody's ever tracked down the other guy," Cissy pointed out. Alicia knew she was referring to a second man the police were looking for in connection to Victor Logan's death. Cissy had filled her in on everything the Cooper family knew about Logan and the events of the previous month, when Logan had taken Cissy's Uncle Jake and his wife Mariah captive.

"Jake's certain the other guy wouldn't have been more than a teenager when your mother was murdered," Gabe said, gently stroking his niece's arm. "I know it doesn't feel like closure. We never got to face Victor Logan and make him admit what he did, but grasping at straws—"

"They may not be straws," Alicia interjected.

Gabe's head snapped toward her. "What is your deal? You're so desperate for a thesis topic that you'd mess with a young girl's mind about her mother's murder?"

"Damn it!" Cissy pulled away from her uncle. "I'm not a baby and Alicia's not messing with my head. Do you have any idea how insulting you're being right now?"

Gabe's expression fell, and he raked his hand through his dark hair, turning away. "I'm sorry."

Alicia crossed to Cissy's side, offering a united front. "Cissy had questions about her mother's murder before she ever stepped foot in my lab. When she found out I was doing my doctoral thesis on a series of unsolved serial murders in the Gulf states, she asked my opinion about her mother's case."

The hard muscles of Gabe's jaws tensed. "My brother and I have both spent the last twelve years looking into every lead that emerged, most of which fell apart. We know a viable suspect when we see one. Victor Logan had the means to do it and the opportunity. And based on his issues with women, we're confident we have a good idea what motivated him—"

"Why you?" Alicia interrupted, struck by something he'd said a moment earlier. "I mean, I get why Cissy's father would have devoted his life to finding an answer, but why you?"

Gabe glanced at his niece before answering. "I'm the one who found her body."

Alicia glanced at Cissy, whose expression was solemn and tinged with sympathy as she gazed up at her uncle. If she found the answer as incomplete as Alicia did, she gave no sign of it.

"I see," she said, although she didn't really. Finding the body might have given Gabe a bigger stake in learning what happened to Cissy's mother, but not enough to spend twelve years following leads long after the case had grown stone-cold.

"I appreciate that you have a paper to write. And I get that having Cissy here is like a case study practically falling into your lap. But all the authorities who've ever looked into Brenda's murder are convinced that Victor Logan is the guy."

"He's one of them," Alicia agreed.

Gabe's brow furrowed. "One of them?"

"I've managed to get my hands on the bulk of the police reports dealing with Victor Logan's actions from this past April as well as your sister-in-law's statements about his actions four years ago, when he killed her son's father." She felt a ripple of guilt at the look of dismay in Gabe's eyes, as if he saw her actions as intrusive and presumptuous.

Maybe he was right. Maybe it wasn't her place. But if her theory was correct, then the nightmare wasn't over.

More women were going to die.

"Uncle Gabe, please listen to her." Cissy put her hand on her uncle's arm. "I didn't want to believe it, either. I was hoping Alicia would tell me I was imagining things."

Gabe's eyes narrowed as he looked from Cissy to Alicia. "I take it you didn't?"

"Why don't we sit?" Alicia motioned toward the sofa.

Gabe frowned but sat. Cissy dropped onto the sofa next to him, leaving Alicia to take the ottoman again. She cleared her throat and leaned forward to pick up the folder Gabe had set down just before Cissy arrived.

"Cissy's been taking criminology courses since last year," Alicia began, straightening the contents of the file to give her twitchy hands something to do. "One of her courses was Basic Criminal Profiling."

"I profiled Mom's murderer as one of my assignments," Cissy added quietly. "Got an A."

"I'm sure you probably know that profiling is more an art than a science," Alicia continued, trying not to react to the raw intensity of Gabe's gaze, part of her wondering what it would feel like to experience that sort of no-holds-barred focus under more intimate circumstances.

"Understatement," he murmured.

She slanted a look at him. "Legwork solves more cases. I don't dispute that."

"The evidence against Logan was damning," he said simply. "Why keep asking a question that's already been answered?"

"Because the one person we can prove Victor killed was a man. A man against whom he had a personal grudge. I read the statements your brother and sister-in-law gave last month after their ordeal with Logan. He used a gun to subdue them, and even then, he wasn't very good at using it. He's not the person who shot the game warden—that was the other man."

"Uncle Gabe, nothing fits, don't you see?" Cissy turned to Gabe, her expression animated. Alicia watched her warily, aware that the younger woman's personal stakes in the case put her at risk of getting too wrapped up in the outcome of Alicia's project. She had to be careful with Cissy, not let her get any more involved than she was already.

Gabe pressed his lips together in consternation. He looked across at Alicia. "How did you get all this material?"

Alicia looked down at her hands, a little embarrassed. "I used to date one of the local cops. He still does favors for me now and then. He talked his bosses into letting me look into some cold cases that might be connected to the other murders."

"And you sweet-talked them into letting you request records from other law enforcement agencies, right?"

Alicia almost laughed aloud. Sweet talk wasn't one of

her strong suits. Bulldozer was a better description. "Something like that. I used Cissy's profile, tweaked it with my own observations and put out feelers to other departments to see if they had any cases that fit the profile."

"What did you find?"

Alicia couldn't tell if he was interested or just humoring his niece. Either way, it might be her only chance to convince him to listen. She dug through the file for the timeline she'd worked out, speaking as she searched. "I found fifteen murders that I think are connected."

"That many?" He sounded surprised.

"I'm not sure there aren't more," she admitted, finally finding the paper she was looking for. She pulled it from the file and laid it on the table in front of her.

Gabe eyed the paper warily, as if it were about to morph into a cobra or something. Alicia darted a look at Cissy, who returned her gaze with an apologetic shrug.

"I need food," Gabe said.

Alicia blinked, caught off balance. "I could make something—"

"No, I think I'll take my niece out to dinner." Gabe stood, looking down at Cissy.

"Uncle Gabe—"

"I'm not shutting down the conversation," he said. "Just tabling it until I've eaten."

Cissy stood, lifting her chin. "Alicia, would you like to join us?"

Gabe's expression was neutral, but Alicia saw the irritation in his blue eyes. She shook her head. "No, not tonight. I've got a lot of work to sort through. You two go have fun. We can talk tomorrow."

Cissy's lips tightened to a thin line and Alicia could see the family resemblance between her and her uncle. But she didn't argue, following Gabe to the front door.

"I'll call you if we don't get back too late," Cissy told Alicia firmly. "This isn't over."

Alicia closed the door behind them, locking up. She remained by the door a moment, surprised by how empty and large the apartment seemed now that her visitors had left.

Gabe Cooper sure knew how to fill a room with his presence.

She crossed to the sofa and plopped down in the space Gabe had just vacated. The cushion was still warm, and maybe she was just imagining it, but she thought she detected a whiff of testosterone lingering in the air.

She laughed aloud, the sound echoing in the silent apartment. Man, she needed to get out more.

Her laughter faltered a few seconds later, when she heard a furtive scrape coming from the porch outside.

Instantly tense, she grabbed her discarded jacket from the coat tree by the door and pulled the vial of pepper spray from the pocket. It seemed grossly inadequate, but her aluminum bat was in the bedroom, too far away.

There was a window by the front door, which would give her a clear view of the porch, but she couldn't talk herself into moving the curtains aside and taking a look. She settled for the peephole in the door and its fish-eyed view. She saw no sign of movement outside.

And yet, she heard another set of creaking noises, as if someone was walking around on the wooden porch outside.

Stop it, she told herself, backing away from the door. *This isn't some isolated warehouse and you're not really alone.*

But she held on to the pepper spray anyway.

"I CAN'T BELIEVE HOW RUDE you were." Cissy kept her voice low, glancing around the restaurant as if she thought her half-whispered rebuke might cause a scene.

Gabe felt a hint of guilt, but it was eclipsed by annoyance at his niece and, more to the point, the pretty little egghead who'd stirred up Cissy's emotions about her mother's murder. "I prefer to call it direct," he answered tightly.

"Call it whatever you want. It was still uncalled for."

"Know what else is uncalled for? Dragging someone across the state on false pretenses." Gabe gave Cissy a pointed look.

"They weren't false. They were...incomplete."

Gabe fiddled with the salad fork lying beside his water glass. "Victor Logan killed your mother." Even as he spoke the words aloud, doubt nagged at him, making the back of his neck prickle with unease.

"You don't sound as convinced here as you did back at Alicia's place," Cissy murmured.

"You haven't mentioned any of this to your dad, have you?"

Cissy looked horrified. "No! I'm not going to him with anything less than hard evidence. He's been through enough pain over the years trying to find Mom's killer."

"So you called me instead." Not that Cissy could understand just how hard the roller coaster of false leads and dashed hopes had been on him, too. She didn't know just how intimately he was involved in the disaster of that night, how much blame he had earned with his selfish thoughtlessness.

"You've been there for my brother and me, as much as anyone. I knew you'd come if I called." Cissy looked across the table at him, her expression softening. "I trust your judgment about this particular topic."

"Except when I disagree with your theories," he added with an indulgent smile.

She grinned. "Exactly."

The waitress arrived to take their orders. Cissy had

chosen one of the higher-end restaurants in town, although in a place like Millbridge, Alabama, high-end was relative. A snowy linen tablecloth covered the small window-side table where they sat, their seats overlooking a moonlit garden partially obscured by their reflection bouncing back at them on the picture window. The flatware was stainless steel, but clean and shiny, free of nicks and stains.

At least the menu was unpretentious. Home cooking, plenty of options. Gabe selected a steak and vegetable plate, though he wasn't feeling particularly hungry at the moment, thanks to Cissy's ambush.

Cissy ordered cheese fries.

"As the apparent stand-in for your father, I have to tell you that cheese fries are almost completely lacking in nutritional value," he said after the waitress departed.

"Cheese has protein," she defended. "Besides, I'm feeling strangely in need of comfort food."

Reaching across the table, he patted her hand. "That's my fault, isn't it?"

Her brow wrinkled. "Not everything's your fault, you know."

But it was, he thought. More than she realized. "You want to go back there tonight?" he asked. "Finish what we started?"

"Yes," she answered simply.

"What do you know about this Alicia person, anyway? What's her deal?"

Cissy gave him an odd look. "Her deal?"

"What made her decide to look into cold cases in the first place?"

"I don't know, exactly. She was already working on her thesis when I took my first lab with her."

"What kind of labs does she teach?" When Gabe had been in school, the labs he'd attended were usually limited to either the hard sciences or language classes. Of course, he had pretty much avoided the social sciences like the plague. His major had been marine biology, with a focus on freshwater ecosystems. Gave him a head start on figuring out where to find the bass when he was fishing a tournament.

"She's helping the head of the psychology department develop research labs for criminal investigations. For instance, she and another grad student, Marlon, are spending a lot of their time working up a set of protocols to quantify the likelihood of a violence-prone individual to escalate to sadistic murder."

Gabe grimaced. "Tell me you're not helping with that one."

"I'm not. You have to be a senior or a grad student to participate." The waitress arrived with Cissy's cheese fries, assuring Gabe his steak was on the way. Gabe took notice of her this time. She was tall, on the curvy side, with a wide, smiling mouth and eyes the color of dark chocolate. She didn't look like Brenda, but there was something about her that reminded Gabe of his sister-in-law.

What little appetite he'd had fled.

"What's the matter?" Cissy asked after the waitress left.

"Nothing."

Cissy followed his gaze as he tracked the waitress' departure. "She's pretty. A little old for you, though. And I think she was wearing a wedding ring—"

Gabe looked across the table at his niece. "She reminded me of someone."

"Mom?"

"A little," he admitted.

"Not that much. She's just on your mind. She's on mine, too." Cissy picked at the plate of cheese fries in front of her, swirling one thin strip of potato in the gooey sauce. "Some days, I barely remember her, and others, it's like I'm right there, curled up in my bed, listening to her read me a story." A hint of a smile curved her pink lips. "Our favorite was *Sam, Bangs and Moonshine*. So mysterious and adventurous. A good lesson about the consequences of lies, too."

"I'm sorry, sweetheart. You shouldn't have had to go through life without your mama." *I shouldn't have let it happen,* he added silently.

Cissy pushed her plate of cheese fries across the table, an unconscious echo of her mother's habit of offering comfort through the distraction of food. In a family that included five active males under the age of thirty at the time, it had often proved a successful ploy. "I know this may seem like a long shot to you—"

"I just don't know if your father can bear another letdown." Gabe gently pushed the plate back toward her. "I don't know if *I* can."

"You may have to." Cissy met his gaze directly, her expression deadly serious. Gabe realized, in that instant, that his little niece had grown up without his realizing it. How had that happened?

"Why's that?" he asked aloud.

Cissy leaned forward, lowering her voice. "Because the murders are still happening."

THE MOON EMERGED FROM BEHIND a wispy cloud, casting a pale blue glow across the front lawn of the Bellewood Manor Apartments. The real estate website was right—it did look like history come to life. He could almost imagine a parade of silly Southern belles strolling along the length of the porch, flirting and flitting and behaving generally like the weak little sheep they were.

He was safely across the street now, hidden by the limber fronds of a willow tree. He'd taken a chance earlier, walking right up to her front door. He'd been careful to stay out of range of the security peephole, though she would have seen him easily enough had she looked out the window.

But she wouldn't look. For all her hardheaded determination to solve the mystery she'd uncovered, Alicia Solano was scared. Scared she fit the victim profile.

Scared she would be next.

Well, she did fit the profile. She was a curvy brunette with a strong, independent streak just screaming for a take down. Hell, sometimes, he wanted to do it himself.

But that wasn't his job. He was the scout, not the hunter. That was Alex's job.

And Alex didn't take foolish chances.

Alicia wouldn't be the next victim. Not here, surrounded by people who could hear or see something and share it with the cops. The next victim worked at a convenience store on Route 7, a cashier who could go a whole six-hour evening shift without seeing a soul now that the bypass to the interstate was completed, diverting traffic away from the dying store.

She would close up at eleven, no doubt relieved to be done with the mind-numbing shift. Her only thought would be of heading home, her mind already full of the things she had to do before she could finally go to bed and get a well-earned night of sleep before dragging herself to her first morning class.

Useless ponderings, of course. She'd never make it to bed.

She'd never even make it out of the store.

By midnight, she'd be dead.

Chapter Three

She heard footsteps on the front porch.

Alicia looked up from the files spread out in front of her, reaching for the aluminum softball bat she'd fetched from the bedroom. Unlike the previous time, these steps were swift and strong. Two sets, moving at a determined pace.

She rose, her heart pounding. She tightened her grip on the bat until her fingers ached.

The steps were almost at her door.

Stop. Just stop. You live in an apartment building, you hyper-excitable idiot. This isn't where he does his work.

She put the bat down beside the sofa and forced her feet toward the front door, looking through the security peephole. Her body buzzed with relief at the sight of Gabe Cooper's impossibly broad shoulders and stubborn chin distorted by the fish-eye lens.

She waited for his knock before opening the door. He blinked, as if surprised by her quick response.

"Is it all right that we're back?" he asked, not bothering with any sort of customary greeting.

They weren't friends, she reminded herself, nor likely to be. This was business.

"Of course." She backed up, letting him and Cissy inside.

Gabe crossed to the sofa and stopped, looking down at the bat and back up at her. "Worried about intruders?"

Alicia grabbed the bat. "Just seeing if I still have my home run swing," she joked, not wanting him to know how spooked she'd been only moments earlier.

"Cissy told me about the two new murders." Gabe sat on the sofa and gave her a look of pure, stubborn-male challenge. "I'd like to know why you think they're connected to Brenda's."

Alicia felt her own bulldog side snapping inside her head, but she held the beast back as she set the bat carefully aside and sat on the ottoman. Cissy stayed a little apart from the fray, her arms crossed and her gaze watchful. She'd done her part, getting Gabe here to talk to Alicia. But she clearly wasn't going to take Alicia's side against her uncle.

Like Gabe before her, Alicia didn't bother with a preamble. "On January 22nd of this year, a coed named Meredith Linden was working at a television repair shop in Blicksville, about ten miles from here. She did their books, reconciled receipts, that sort of thing, and because she was attending college during the day, she worked at night. She lived off campus in an apartment by herself, so nobody noticed she didn't come home. The owners of the repair shop found her body the next morning. She'd been raped, then stabbed several times, laid on her back and left to die. No fingerprints left, no DNA from the rape."

Gabe met her gaze, unflinching. "Next?"

She felt herself grinding her back teeth. Forcing her jaw to relax, she continued. "On March 12th, Addison Moore was cleaning a small office in Pekoe, out near the railroad tracks. Also a college student, also going to school by day and cleaning at night after the business closed and her classes ended. Her roommate got worried when she didn't show up at ten, as she usually did. She found Addison's body in the first floor lobby, stabbed several times and positioned on her back."

Alicia sat back, glancing from Gabe to Cissy, who gave a small shrug. She looked back at Gabe, who was watching her with slightly narrowed eyes.

"Two dead coeds in similar crime scenes and similar circumstances in the same town is possibly a sign you have a serial killer working here," Gabe conceded, his jaw set in concrete. Alicia could see a spark of triumph in his eyes, as if he'd just proved to himself that his instincts were right, that these recent murders weren't connected to Brenda Cooper's death or the slayings of the other women chronicled in Victor Logan's barbecued scrapbook.

She was pretty sure she knew why Gabe had dismissed her presentation as irrelevant, but she pressed him on the question anyway. "What about the similarities in the killer's M.O.?"

"Ms. Solano, your two coeds have to be a good four or five years younger than any of Victor Logan's victims. Victims in their mid- to late twenties are clearly part of Logan's signature. M.O.s change. Signatures don't. I'd think someone doing her dissertation on serial killers would know that already."

She ignored the mild condescension, because she had him exactly where she wanted him. "They weren't four or five years younger. Meredith Linden was twenty-eight. Addison Moore was twenty-nine. Both brunettes, just like the other victims. Curvy women, like the others."

Gabe's eyes shifted, his gaze dropping to her body as if searching for her own curves. They were camouflaged by the plain skirt and loose-fitting blouse she'd chosen from her closet this morning, but she could tell he was seeing beyond the shapeless clothing and picturing what lay below.

"Now do you understand?" Cissy asked her uncle.

He looked at her, his brow wrinkled. "There's never

been any evidence in Brenda's murder that would suggest a second killer, Cissy. Evidence matters, too."

"There aren't two killers," Alicia said. "Just one."

Gabe swung his puzzled gaze her way. "You said you thought Victor was *one* of the killers."

"He's not one of the killers. Just one of the people involved." Alicia could see his skepticism growing. "Look, Cissy says you're a deputy, so I know you probably know this—sometimes there are serial killer pairs. Some of the time they both kill, but sometimes, the weaker of the two—the beta—only aids the killer by doing things like taking care of his kit or acting as a lookout. And sometimes, they just help the killer stalk the victims to pick the right time to strike. I think that was the case for Victor Logan. And I think now our killer has a new wingman."

"Interesting theory." He cut his eyes toward his niece. "Not one I find particularly plausible, but—"

"I don't need you to believe it," Alicia conceded grudgingly, although a little openness to hearing her theories would have been nice. "I just need—"

"Yeah, that's another thing I've been wondering," Gabe interrupted. "What do you need me for? Cissy probably knows everything I know about the murders. Maybe more, since she's apparently been making them a subject of study."

Alicia looked up at Cissy, an apology in her eyes. "Cissy doesn't know what it was like to find Brenda's body. *You* do. And that's why I need to talk to you."

Gabe shook his head quickly. "I'm not rehashing all of that with you. Certainly not with Cissy here."

"I've read your statement to the Chickasaw County deputies," Cissy said.

He looked up at his niece, his expression wary. "It's not the same as hearing it."

"Actually, what I'm hoping we can do is go a step beyond your statement," Alicia said, her stomach tightening into a fist-sized knot. What she was going to suggest was invasive under the best of circumstances, and this definitely wasn't the best of circumstances. "I think we should try hypnotic regression."

Gabe's hard gaze whipped around to flood her with molten fury. "You're nuts."

"Uncle Gabe—" Cissy warned.

Gabe pushed to his feet. "You want to play some sort of mind game with me so you can make a nice score on your paper? Too bad. I'm not playing. I'm done here." He moved around the coffee table and strode angrily toward the door.

Cissy caught up with him before Alicia. "I know it's a lot to ask, and I know it's not something a lot of people are comfortable taking part in—"

Gabe interrupted with a hard laugh. "I hope you and Ms. Solano find what you're looking for. I really do. But you're going to have to count me out."

Alicia caught Cissy's arm when she was about to argue further. "Thank you for hearing me out," she said sincerely. It was more than she'd had a right to hope for. "I'm sure Cissy will be in touch if we find anything new your brother needs to know about. And if you think of anything, here's my card." She pulled one of her business cards from the desk near the door, handing it to Gabe.

He tucked it into his pocket.

Alicia unlocked the front door and opened it for him. "Thank you," she said again.

"I'll walk you to the truck," Cissy suggested.

Gabe turned to look at her, his brow furrowed. "No. You go home, lock the doors and be safe. I may not think your mother's killer is still at work around here, but someone is. You be careful." To Alicia's surprise, Gabe's blistering blue gaze turned to meet hers, softening as he dropped his voice a tone. "You, too." His eyes dropped, taking in her well-camouflaged figure as if he could see right through her clothes.

Heat rose in her cheeks. "Will do."

Then he was gone, broad shoulders and long legs disappearing into the darkening night.

"I'm sorry," Cissy murmured. "I guess I knew it would be a long shot."

Alicia gave the taller girl a hug. "He's right, though. Go home. Get some sleep. Lock your doors."

She watched until Cissy was safely inside the apartment two doors down, then stepped back into her own place and locked the doors behind her.

Gabe Cooper had looked her over. More than once. So he'd seen it, too. The obvious.

She walked slowly into her bedroom and unbuttoned her blouse, letting the garment slide to her feet. Next came the skirt, left where it lay as she crossed to her closet door and looked at her reflection in the full-length mirror bolted to the door. Her dark eyes stared back, wide with the anxiety she tried to hide from the world.

The woman in the mirror had full breasts and wide hips that even her shapeless clothing couldn't completely hide, courtesy of her father's side of the family. Three times a week at the gym gave her muscles beneath the flesh, but it couldn't change her DNA. She was a curvy woman.

And she perfectly fit the killer's profile.

GABE TURNED UP THE RADIO as Lynyrd Skynyrd's "Simple Man" came on. Like a lot of classic rock stations in the South, on this station, southern fried rock got a lot of air-play, and Skynyrd was one of Gabe's favorites.

He sang along under his breath as he navigated the winding curves of Route 7. The two-lane county road undulated northeast, away from downtown Millbridge and the Mill Valley University campus and out toward the rural wilds that encroached the town on all sides.

He'd taken a room at a small budget motel situated on the county road near the delineation between town and country, somehow leery of staying closer to campus, where the relentless beat of a college town's energy might pose too dark a reminder of his own youthful follies.

But after the night he'd just spent dealing with his stubborn niece and her even more bullheaded teacher, he sort of regretted the miles still standing between him and a long, hot shower and a good night's sleep.

He should have known Cissy was up to something. His niece was a sweet girl, but she had taken to college life like a hound dog to a 'possum chase, reveling in her freedom and the responsibilities that came with being on her own. No way she'd have invited a visit from her uncle unless she wanted something more than just a friendly ear and a free dinner.

Not that it mattered. He'd do anything his niece asked. It was the least he owed her. His selfish inattention had led to Cissy and her brother Mike spending the last twelve years motherless. If Gabe had arrived at the trucking company on time, he might have stopped Victor Logan. Then, not only would Brenda be alive, but God knew how many other women Logan had killed might be with their families as well.

All because he'd wanted to have a beer and a game of pool with an old high school friend.

As the song on the radio changed to something slow and bluesy, Gabe's cell phone buzzed. He glanced at the display. It was Cissy.

He turned down the radio and answered. "Hey, Cissy. What's up?"

"I just wanted to talk to you before I go to bed. I know you're mad at me—"

"I'm not mad."

"You should be. I should have told you everything up front instead of dragging you here for the ambush."

"I wouldn't have come if you hadn't set up the ambush," he admitted, spotting the Route 7 Motor Lodge sign glowing faintly orange in the distance.

"I know, but it wasn't fair of me to do it anyway."

"Well, no harm done. Maybe I'll get a little fishing done in the area before I leave tomorrow. That'll be worth it." He lowered his voice conspiratorially. "What say you cut some classes and come fishing with your Uncle Gabe, just like old times?"

Cissy's laugh was damp with emotion. "Not this time. End of year exams coming, you know."

"Yeah, you're your daddy's daughter," he teased gently. "Little Miss Responsible."

My opposite, he added mentally, his smile fading.

He had almost reached the motel. "Well, you get a good night's sleep and kick butt tomorrow in class."

Cissy giggled. "Will do." She hung up.

Gabe disconnected and laid the phone on the seat beside him. He was only a few yards from the motel parking lot entrance, but he found his foot remaining settled over the accelerator. He passed the motel and kept going.

He checked the dashboard clock. Almost eleven. As he was driving in earlier today, he'd noticed a convenience store sitting all by itself on the side of Route 7. It wouldn't close before eleven, would it? He could grab some snacks to get him through the night, since his barely-touched dinner was a distant memory.

Past the motel, he was solidly into wilderness, hemmed by trees on either side and ahead of him as far as the eye could see. He'd passed few vehicles on the road at this time of night, so the sudden glare of headlights coming around a curve ahead made him wince. The other driver dropped his bright lights. Gabe did the same and they passed on the narrow road.

With an empty road ahead, Gabe put the headlights on bright again, driving some of the shadows to the edges of the road. He drove about a half mile further along the winding rural road before the lights of the Stiller's Food and Fuel came into view.

There was only one car parked at the convenience store, a small Honda Civic that had seen better years. It was parked around the side. Probably belonged to the clerk inside.

He parked in front and pocketed his keys and cell phone. As he opened the door, a bell jingled, announcing his arrival. But nobody stood at the counter, nor did anyone come running at the sound of the bell. Curious, but not alarmed, Gabe grabbed a shopping basket and headed down the snack aisle to contemplate his choices.

Beef jerky, smoked almonds, packs of string cheese from the refrigerator section—he threw all of these into the blue plastic basket. He debated the barbecue pork rinds for a moment before tossing them into the basket as well. He bypassed beer and soft drinks and went straight to the juices— apple, grape and orange juice went into the basket.

He spotted a fishing magazine on a rack near the front and picked it up. He had this issue at home but hadn't had a chance to read it. If the night got long, he could fill the time with this, he decided, topping off the basket with the magazine.

The cashier's desk remained empty as he approached. He looked around, wondering if he'd just missed someone stocking shelves somewhere else in the store. But he saw no one.

"Hello?" His voice seemed to echo in the empty store.

He glanced back at the door. The "Closed" sign faced him, so the "Open" sign was still facing the outside.

"Hello?" he called again.

The silence that answered seemed to swallow him whole.

He set the basket on the counter and leaned over to look behind it. There was no one lying injured or dead behind it. But a strange, sinking sensation in Gabe's belly made him keep looking.

There was a back room behind the counter; Gabe could see the door to it standing barely ajar down past the cigarette kiosk. The back room was accessible only from behind the counter, and the counter was walled off with a latched door that wouldn't budge when Gabe tried to open it.

It wasn't tall enough to pose an obstacle, however. He jumped over the door and landed behind the counter, a few feet from the back room door.

Hair prickled wildly on the back of his neck, but he forced himself forward. "Hello?" he called again, giving the unlatched door a light push. It swung open with a loud, groaning creak.

The light was off in the back room, hiding most of the area from Gabe's view. He felt along the wall until he located a switch and gave it a flick.

Yellow light from a single bald bulb filled the room with a muddy glow, revealing what the shadows had hidden.

A woman lay on the floor, her legs stretched out and her hands flat on the floor by her side. Her clothes were neatly in place and her eyes were closed. But across her belly, a series of bloody puncture wounds marred the pale gray of her blouse.

For a second, Gabe was no longer in the middle of a convenience store back room. Instead he was in the woods of Chickasaw County, only a few yards from the trucking company where Brenda had worked, staring down at the bloodstained body of his sister-in-law.

He forced himself to touch the store clerk's throat to check for a pulse, knowing what he'd find as surely as he knew his own name.

This killer wasn't going to leave behind a live victim. He never had before.

Gabe pulled his cell phone from his pocket and dialed 911.

Then he pulled out the card still resting in his back pocket. The one Alicia Solano had handed him before she let him out of her apartment.

Alicia answered on the third ring, her voice raspy and alarmed.

"It's Gabe Cooper," he said tersely, not bothering with small talk, since he knew she wouldn't want it. "There's been another murder."

"What?" She sounded more awake now, and over the phone, he heard the rustle of fabric, as if she were throwing on a robe. Gabe was tempted to let himself dwell on the picture that rose to mind at that thought, if only to drive out the sight of the dead woman lying at his feet.

He'd give almost anything to get that image out of his head.

"I stopped at a convenience store on Route 7—Stiller's Food and Fuel," he said aloud. "Nobody came to ring me up, so I looked for the cashier. I found her in a back room. Dead. It's the same guy, Alicia."

"As the other two coed murders?" she asked carefully.

"As all of them," he answered, his gaze drawn back to the murderer's handiwork. "All of Victor Logan's murders.

Or the ones he helped facilitate," he added, giving in to the probability that Alicia's theory was right. "Alicia, this guy's still killing. And you're right. We have to stop him."

Chapter Four

It was almost two o'clock in the morning before Gabe Cooper knocked on Alicia's door. She'd spent the hours since his call on her sofa, certain she'd be unable to sleep. But the long day at work and her stressful evening had taken a toll on her stamina. Gabe's knock woke her from a dead sleep.

She pushed to a sitting position on the sofa where she'd nodded off, taking a second to gain control over her jangling nerves. Tightening her robe over the shorts and tank top she wore as pajamas, she pushed to her feet. After a quick check of the peephole, she unlocked the door and let Gabe inside.

He looked haggard and apologetic. "I should have just gone back to the motel instead. It's so late—"

She took his arm and led him to the sofa. "No, I want to hear everything you want to tell me. I guess you've been with the cops?"

Gabe's hair already looked as if he'd spent the last few hours running his hands through it. Another pass didn't do anything to improve its disheveled state. "Yeah. They had a lot of questions."

She hadn't even considered they might think him a suspect. "They didn't arrest you or anything, did they?"

"No. They called my brother Aaron, who's a deputy

sheriff back home. He vouched for me. That seemed to be good enough for the locals."

"This is so weird. Your just dropping by that particular convenience store at that particular time—"

"Yeah, I think the cops were pretty struck by that, too. But it's less than a mile up the road from my motel, and I hadn't eaten much dinner, so I went to stock up on some snacks." Gabe grimaced. "Not really that hungry anymore."

Her chest ached with sympathy. He looked so tired. "You know, maybe what you really need is sleep. We can talk about this tomorrow—"

Gabe shook his head. "It's fresh in my head now. Best time to discuss it."

"Okay. How do you want to start? Just tell me what happened, start to finish? Or skip to the details?"

"Nothing really happened—I went to the store, shopped for the food, and by the time I got to the counter, nobody had responded to the bell over the door that rang when I arrived." Gabe's blue eyes met hers suddenly. "Can I have some water?"

"Of course." Alicia kicked herself mentally for not offering something when he first arrived. She found a large glass and filled it with water, adding extra ice because she'd seen the way he'd eyed the glass earlier that evening with a mixture of amusement and mild disappointment. Southerners seemed to like an inordinate amount of ice in their beverages.

He took the glass from her. "Extra ice," he murmured, a small smile curving the edges of his mouth.

She smiled back. "I guess you earned it."

He cradled the glass between his large hands. "It was so quiet. I called out, thinking maybe the clerk was in the back and hadn't heard the bell, but there was no answer."

"So you went into the back?"

He nodded. "The back room was dark, but I could feel her. When I turned on the light, I knew exactly what I'd see."

The haggard look in his eyes when he lifted his gaze to meet hers made her breath catch. She reached across and covered his hand with her own.

He looked down at her hand, slowly turning his own until his palm touched hers. "I know you told me the signatures were similar, but when I saw her lying there—" He broke off, seeming unable to find the words.

She waited in silence, realizing Gabe Cooper was dealing with a lot more than just finding a dead body this evening. He'd found Brenda Cooper's body, too. He'd been younger than Alicia was now, no more than twenty-one or twenty-two. It might well have been the first time he'd ever seen a dead body outside a funeral home. And now, it had happened again.

Gabe cleared his throat, finally, and finished his thought. "It was like finding Brenda's body all over again. The pose, the wounds, the woman's shape and overall looks." His gaze slanted toward her. "You fit the profile, Alicia. You have to know that."

She nodded.

"You have to be really careful, do you understand?"

"I know," she agreed. She'd thought of little else since she'd first realized just how much she looked like the previous two victims and, if Gabe's reaction were anything to go by, the third victim as well. "Did you get a name for the victim?"

"Melanie Phelps."

Alicia gave a small start. Melanie Phelps was in one of her psych classes. "I know her. About twenty-seven, shoulder-length dark brown hair, brown eyes—"

Gabe nodded. "This guy is a lot more specific than I ever really gave him credit for being."

"How would you have known?" she asked sensibly. "You knew about Brenda, and after the fact, you learned about the other women in Mississippi and Alabama, but with the scrapbook practically destroyed, you couldn't have tracked those people down and made the connections."

"How did you do it?" Gabe asked, waving his hand at the folder still lying on her coffee table. "You've already connected these murders to previous murders, including Brenda's. How'd you even know where to look?"

She listened for any hint of suspicion or skepticism in Gabe's voice, but all she heard was curiosity. "It started with a favor I was doing for a friend. He's a police officer, and he'd been the first officer on the scene at Meredith Linden's murder—the one at the TV repair shop in Blicksville. Anyway, he went to college in Livingston, and there was a case there that had been a big deal in town, and Tony—my friend—thought Meredith Linden's case sounded suspiciously similar."

"So he asked you to work your profiling mojo?"

She bit back a smile. "Something like that. I went with the premise that there had to be other similar murders, unsolved, since the guy was still killing. I started gathering information on unsolved murders in Alabama and Mississippi. Anyway, sometime last month, Cissy came to me—she'd heard about my side project, since by then I was thinking seriously about making it the topic of my dissertation, and I wasn't exactly being secretive about it. She told me about Victor Logan and his scrapbook."

"And Brenda's murder?"

She nodded. "The M.O. was so similar—curvy, dark-haired, dark-eyed woman in her mid- to late twenties, working alone late at night in a secluded area. Raped, then stabbed to death." She held back a shudder. "I started searching through cold cases for that victim profile, making a list of possible victims based on characteristics the killer might find appealing—body shape, hair color, eye color, type of job—that sort of thing."

"The convenience store was in the middle of nowhere," Gabe said quietly. "Melanie Phelps could have gone her whole shift without seeing anyone. Just like Brenda."

Alicia nodded, not missing the bleak tone of his voice. He'd clearly taken his sister-in-law's murder hard. She wondered if there was more to it than his being the person who found her. "Did the police get anything from the security tape at the convenience store?" she asked aloud.

Gabe released a soft huff of grim laughter. "All the tapes were missing. The guy apparently knew what to look for and covered his tracks."

Alicia grimaced. "He's been at it a long time. He's probably only getting better at it as he goes."

"You know what? I shouldn't have come here. I gave the police a statement. It's probably going to be more accurate than anything that I can come up with right now." Rubbing his temples, Gabe stood. "I should just go back to the motel and let you get some sleep. I can ask to see my statement tomorrow and refresh my memory then."

Alicia caught him as he started toward the door. "Wait. Don't go."

He stopped and looked down, towering over her. The room around them seemed to close in on all sides, heat roiling the air between them. Alicia dropped her hand away from his arm, but her fingers still tingled from the feel of his sinewy muscles beneath her fingertips.

"What?" he asked, his voice little more than a murmur.

"You can take my bed. I'll sleep on the sofa."

His eyes narrowed slightly at her blurted offer, and her cheeks grew hot with embarrassment. Had she really just invited a stranger to stay the night?

"I think the killer's probably through for the night. You should be safe," Gabe said.

She was tempted to latch onto the easy out he'd just given her, but that wasn't really why she'd asked him to stay. Sure, having him around would make her feel exponentially less vulnerable, but so would a German shepherd.

"That's not what I mean," she said, stepping away from him to try to regain her focus. "I just—you came here because of me, and you've had a rough night because of me. The least I can do is give you somewhere homey and nice to stay instead of some Route 7 motel room."

"The motel's not so bad," he said. But she could tell the words were perfunctory.

She turned back to look at him. "I make a mean omelet."

His lips curved. "Now you're playing dirty."

"And, okay," she admitted, "I *would* feel a little safer if someone else was here tonight."

He laid one large hand on her shoulder, the touch gentle and undemanding. Still, the flesh beneath her robe tingled and burned as if he'd caressed her. "I'll take the sofa."

She eyed the brightly colored sofa warily, feeling a little guilty at the idea of his spending the night hunched up there, trying to make his long limbs fit. "It's not very big."

"It'll do." He dropped his hand away from her shoulder and sat on the sofa, hunching forward to rub his face. His palms swished audibly against the rough patch of beard growth shadowing his jaw. "I'm keeping you up. You probably have classes in the morning or something."

"I have a lab at eleven," she answered softly, surprised by how much willpower it was taking not to snuggle up next to him on the sofa. Where had this sudden susceptibility to big biceps and sexy blue eyes come from?

She was a career woman. Dating was a sporadic thing for her, worked in around classes and studies. She'd tried dating entirely outside the criminology pool, which ended in disaster. Then she'd tried dating a cop—not quite a disaster, but no happy ending there, either. She couldn't give the time or attention required to nurture a long-term relationship.

Recently, she'd stopped trying.

"Why criminology?" Gabe's voice rumbled into the middle of her musings. She found him looking up at her, curiosity tinting his blue eyes with hints of smoky gray.

"Why not?" she countered lightly, not sure she really wanted to get into the whole sordid Solano family saga at this time of night.

"My brother Aaron became a deputy after he was arrested for toilet-papering a neighbor's house," Gabe answered, leaning back and threading his fingers together behind his head. "Well, not immediately after. In between, he blew out his knee, ending a promising college and maybe pro football career. That might have had something to do with it, too."

"Probably." She dropped to the ottoman, trying not to stare too obviously at the lovely things his taut chest muscles were doing to the front of his gray polo shirt. What had they been talking about? Oh, right—criminology and why she'd chosen it as a career. She squelched the urge to fan her hot cheeks.

"My brother-in-law, Riley, became a cop because he didn't want to be a rancher, so when his best friend became a cop, Riley figured, why not?" Gabe's eyes narrowed slightly, watching her through the space between his ridiculously long, dark lashes. "Which brings me back to you. How did a nice girl from San Francisco end up in Millbridge, Alabama, investigating murders in the first place?"

She smiled down at him. "It's a long story, and we both need a little sleep. So how about this? I go get you a pillow and a blanket, and in the morning, over that omelet I promised, I'll tell you the story of Alicia Solano, girl detective. Sound like a plan?"

The sleepy-eyed look he gave her almost made her knees buckle. For a second, any thought beyond dragging him back to her bedroom with her fled her mind. But she managed to get a grip on her hormones before she did something stupid and headed out of the room in search of bedding.

In the hall closet she found a spare pillow and a thin cotton blanket which should offer just enough cover in this warm climate. She pulled them out and held them tightly against the front of her robe, taking a couple of bracing breaths before she returned to the living room.

Okay, add "sexy Southern men" to the list of "things that make Alicia lose her head and behave like a blithering idiot," she thought. Not that any of the other men around here had ever had quite such a potent effect on her equilibrium before.

He wasn't even her type. He had to be in his mid-thirties, putting him nearly a decade older than she was. She'd never been one to find older men particularly attractive.

Yeah, but those older men didn't look like Gabe Cooper, chica.

She took no small amount of pride in the steadiness of her gait as she took the bedding back into the living room. Gabe was in the kitchen, refilling his glass of water. He'd stripped off the polo shirt he'd been wearing earlier, revealing a plain white T-shirt beneath.

Alicia held back a whimper when he came around the kitchen counter into the living room, revealing just how tightly the soft cotton hugged his muscular arms and shoulders. She dropped the bedding on the sofa and retreated to the kitchen for her own glass of water.

She gulped it down greedily, keeping her back to the living room. She ventured a quick glance over her shoulder. "Do you need another pillow or a heavier blanket?"

"No, this will be fine." Gabe's muscles flexed as he unfolded the blanket and laid it over the back of the sofa.

By the time Alicia returned to the living room, he was sitting on the sofa with one boot off, busily untying the string of the other boot. "When I was a kid, we used to go camping in the woods up on Gossamer Ridge—it's the mountain behind our house. I have five brothers and a sister, and the whole crew would go—even Hannah, who was the baby." He grinned up at her, clearly caught up in the memory, and Alicia sank to the ottoman before her legs gave out on her.

"Big family, huh?" Her voice sounded faint and raspy, but if Gabe noticed, he gave no sign.

"Yeah, and getting bigger all the time. Aaron's getting married next month, and Luke and Abby just found out she's expecting. There'll be Coopers running all over Gossamer Ridge for generations to come. I reckon most of them will go camping during the summers, too." He waved at the sofa beneath him. "Won't have a bed quite this comfortable, though."

"You're just saying that to make me feel like less of a hostess failure."

He grinned at her, and her legs went gelid. "Did you ever go camping? There are some great places near San Francisco for hiking and camping."

She laughed aloud at the thought. "My parents were about as far from the camping type as you get. We spent our spare time at museums, libraries and rallies."

"Well, that can be fun, too," he murmured, kicking off his other shoe. She couldn't tell whether he was sincere or just humoring her.

"Sure, but a little camping might have been fun once in a while," she grumbled. "Just for variety."

"Tell you what. Next time you and Cissy have a break at school, get her to take you up to Gossamer Ridge and I'll see how many Coopers we can gather together for a camping trip." He stripped off his socks and folded them on top of the polo shirt sitting on the coffee table. "Maybe we'll even take you on the haunted hike."

She could tell by his tone of voice that he was enticing her into asking the obvious question. But as much as she wanted to know exactly what a haunted hike was, she resisted. Despite her later class schedule, she still wanted to get up early and do some more work on her thesis. And Gabe looked as if he'd just run a marathon uphill. They both needed sleep.

"I might take you up on that if I ever finish my thesis." She stood, flattening her robe where it had bunched from sitting. "But for now, I have plans to work in the morning before my classes, and you can certainly use a little sleep—"

"Wait." Gabe's hand snaked out to circle her wrist. Almost instantly, her whole arm went tingly and hot. "You said you think I should try hypnotic regression, to remember more about what happened the night of Brenda's murder. I think it's worth a shot. Do you know anyone here who could do it? Maybe set me up with someone—"

"Actually, I'm a licensed hypnotherapist," she answered, forcing her voice past the growing lump in her throat. "I could do it."

"You?" His eyes narrowing, he released her arm. She

tucked her wrist against her belly, resisting the urge to rub the burning skin where he'd touched her.

"After I got my masters in psychology, I did the course work necessary to earn my license. I thought it might be a handy skill if I continued with my criminology work."

He gazed up at her, bemused. "Just how old are you, anyway?"

She lifted her chin. "Twenty-five."

"So young." Gabe laid his head against the back of the sofa and closed his eyes. "Man, this has turned out to be a hell of a night."

She eyed him with sympathy. "Not quite what you bargained for when you took Cissy's call, huh?"

He turned his face toward her, opening his eyes. "You haven't told her about the new murder, have you?"

She shook her head. "It can wait until morning."

"I wish I could spare her altogether."

"You can't. She has even more of an investment in getting to the truth than you do. You know that."

"Yeah." He didn't sound happy about it.

Alicia resisted the temptation to smooth back the unruly dark hair spilling onto his forehead. He looked like a tired little boy. The events of the night had obviously gotten to him. "Get some sleep," she suggested. "We'll try to make sense of everything in the morning."

"I'm not sure that's possible." Gabe looked up at her again. "Thanks, Alicia. For all of this. I wasn't nice to you earlier and you had every right to hang up when I called you tonight. I appreciate the second chance."

She felt a strange curling sensation in the pit of her belly. "Thanks for giving me a second chance, too. I'm hoping we'll learn some new things about Brenda's murder once you've had a chance to go back and take a fresh look."

"It may not work," he warned. "I don't like thinking back to that time. My subconscious may be just as resistant."

"We'll worry about that when we get there," she answered firmly, even as she acknowledged what he was saying. Gabe had stumbled onto a scene that had upended the life of his brother, his niece and nephew, and his whole family. She wouldn't blame him if he never wanted to remember that moment again.

But they had to try. If there was anything hidden in Gabe's subconscious that could help unlock the mystery of the alpha killer, she had to take a shot at unearthing it.

"ARE WE SURE THIS IS A GOOD idea?" Gabe eyed the locket in Alicia's hands, mesmerized by the dull gold patina. He felt strangely drugged, already, as if just the sight of that locket were enough to drag him into the bowels of his subconscious.

"It's a great idea," she reassured him, leaning toward him until he could see down her light gray blouse. Inside was all shadows and temptation. He found a new object of fascination.

There was a pounding sound in his ears. His pulse, perhaps, beating at a rapid-fire cadence, driven by the surge of blood gathering in his gut and lower. He tried to ignore the sound, preferring to concentrate on picturing the firm curves hidden in the lacy caress of the lavender bra he could see peeking from beneath her unbuttoned blouse.

But the sound wouldn't go away. He looked away from her breasts, his gaze lifting to meet her dark eyes.

But the face before him wasn't Alicia Solano's. The eyes were equally dark, but lifeless and fixed. Instead of Alicia's creamy olive skin, this face was encased in tight flesh as pale as the grave. Colorless lips parted to reveal crimson-tinted teeth, slick with blood.

Gabe jerked upright, his head pounding. The room was already growing bright with the approach of day, early morning sunlight slanting through the bright red curtains covering the window across from the sofa. In that first, waking moment, he was utterly convinced someone had sneaked past him in the night and murdered Alicia in her bed.

So powerful was the conviction that he'd made it as far as her bedroom door before he caught himself. He looked down at his watch. Only a little after six o'clock. They'd been up past two the night before.

She might be dead asleep, but she wasn't dead.

He returned to the living room, any hope of getting back to sleep now gone. Instead, he pulled out his phone and dialed the one person he knew would be up this early.

"Where the hell are you?" his twin, Jake, answered without as much as a greeting.

"Still in Millbridge," he answered, grinning at the sound of his brother's voice. "How's the fishing?"

"Started out fast, but already slowing down. I'm sure my client is thrilled that I'm talking on the phone to my brother while I should be imparting my superior bass angling expertise."

Gabe heard a very feminine snort on the other end of the line. "Is that your wife?" he asked.

"I didn't say she was a paying client."

"Hi, Gabe," Mariah Cooper called out.

"Hi, Mariah."

Jake passed along the greeting. "So, what was this mysterious something Cissy wanted with you?"

Gabe caught his brother up on all that had happened in the last twelve hours, relieved to share it all with someone who understood how painful Brenda's death had been to him. "It was like living it over again. Almost everything, except the setting, was like that night. It was creepy and disturbing."

"You haven't told J.D. any of this, have you?"

"No," Gabe assured his brother. "You can't, either."

The sound of footsteps on the porch outside Alicia's apartment put Gabe on instant alert. "Jake, I'll call you back," he said quietly. He flipped the phone closed and pushed to his feet, moving quietly across the hardwood floor on bare feet. He stopped at the door, peering through the fish-eye lens.

A sandy-haired man rose from a crouch, gazing right into the lens.

Jake knew the moment he threw the deadbolt, he'd lose the element of surprise. So he went for speed instead, whipping open the lock and jerking the door open.

The sandy-haired man froze, staring at Gabe.

"Who the hell are you?" they demanded in unison.

Chapter Five

The man standing on the porch seemed more surprised to see Gabe than Gabe was to see him. His eyes narrowed as Gabe blocked the doorway with his body.

"It's six o'clock. What are you doing sneaking around the porch at this hour?" Gabe pressed. "What's your name?"

The young man's pointed chin lifted. "What's yours?"

Gabe had a couple of inches on the younger man, and at least twenty pounds, but all of that advantage could be negated by a weapon. He gave the man a once-over, checking for any sign of a hidden gun or knife. Fortunately, the stranger was dressed for jogging, in a snugly-fitting gray T-shirt and a pair of running shorts that didn't have enough room to hide a weapon.

Gabe dropped his guard, marginally. "Gabe Cooper," he answered the other man's question. "Your turn."

The man's lips pressed to a tight line. "Marlon Dyson."

"What's that?" Gabe nodded toward the plastic jewel case lying on the porch at Marlon's feet.

Marlon looked down. "Something for Alicia. Is she here?" He craned his neck to look past Gabe into the apartment.

"She's sleeping," Gabe answered. "She had a long night."

One of Marlon's sandy-brown eyebrows notched upward,

and Gabe realized what sort of impression he'd just given the other man. But before he could decide whether or not to correct the supposition, footsteps padded across the floor behind him, and Alicia's sleep-raspy voice sent a ripple of heat flooding into his lower abdomen.

"Marlon? What are you doing here this early?"

Gabe turned to look at her, putting himself squarely between her and Marlon. He tried not to stare, but it was damned near impossible to drag his eyes away from her. She was still wrapped in that terry cloth robe that looked like it had been purchased for someone twice her size, but enough of the robe gaped open to give him a good look at the shadowy cleft between her firm, round breasts and a very tantalizing peek at the curve of her thigh.

Marlon's voice behind him gave him just enough of a cold splash of reality to control the stirring of his body.

"I was up early, watching the local news, and they teased something about a murder. I had a hunch, so I recorded it." Marlon reached down and picked up the jewel case he'd put on the porch. "I think it may be another one of those murders."

Gabe shot Alicia a quizzical look.

"Gabe, this is Marlon Dyson. We share lab duties for a couple of classes in the psych department. Marlon, this is Gabe Cooper. I think you probably know his niece, Cissy, from your abnormal psychology labs—tall, dark hair, smart as a whip?"

Marlon's brow furrowed. "Oh. Right."

Gabe could tell the introduction didn't really answer Marlon's main question—what was Gabe doing at her apartment at six in the morning, while she was still dressed in her fuzzy robe and looking sexy and sleepy at the same time?

"Anyway—" Marlon cleared his throat, taking a step

back toward the porch stairs. "I was out running and thought I'd drop the DVD by."

"Shouldn't you leave the DVD?" Gabe asked.

Marlon's face flushed lightly, but he picked up the jewel case and held out the DVD toward Alicia. Gabe took it from him, making Marlon frown.

"Thanks, Marlon. I'll take a look at the newscast," Alicia answered, her tone gentle. She took the DVD from Gabe's hand and gave him a fierce look of warning.

Gabe felt a little guilty—for all he knew, Marlon and Alicia had something going on together. She and her lab partner were close to the same age, probably shared a lot of interests in common.

But the guy was such an obvious poser, with his too-long hair flopping down in his face like a pop-star wannabe and his stupid little soul patch growing like a fungus under his bottom lip. What could Alicia possibly see in a jerk like that?

"See you at eleven?" Marlon asked, craning his head to see past Gabe.

"At eleven." She raised a hand in a wave, and Marlon headed down the porch stairs. Gabe pushed the door closed and locked it firmly behind him, turning to look at her.

"What the hell was that?" she asked.

"What?" He pretended ignorance, although he knew exactly what she was asking.

"If I want a Rottweiler, I know where the animal shelter is." She waved her hand at the door. "I don't need to be protected from the people I work with."

"What if you do?" Gabe leaned against the door, folding his arms across his chest. "We don't know who's behind these killings."

"I'm pretty sure it's not Marlon. He would barely have been a teenager when the first killings took place."

Gabe wasn't so sure. Teenagers were capable of some fairly heinous things. And besides, they weren't just talking about one killer here. "You think the alpha killer has picked up a new partner, right?"

She frowned. "Yes, but—"

Gabe pushed away from the door and walked toward her. "Everybody's a suspect, Alicia."

"Even you?"

He stopped midstride. "I guess you should consider all possibilities, even that one."

To his relief, she didn't even look conflicted by the notion. She'd apparently made up her mind about him. He supposed she'd seen too much of his guilt and grief firsthand last night to even consider him as a possible suspect.

"When do you want to try the hypnosis?" she asked, changing the subject.

A shiver of dread ran through him, but he lifted his chin and steeled his spine. "How about this morning?"

She looked surprised by his answer. "I don't know—"

"How long will it take?"

"Not long," she admitted. "At least, not any one session."

He frowned at the thought. "Exactly how many sessions do you foresee?"

Her eyes narrowed. "I don't know how long it'll take to break through to your memory of that night. It could happen quickly or it could take multiple sessions. There's no way to know until we do it."

His jaw squared. "Then the sooner we start, the better."

She stared at him a moment, her eyes narrowed as if she were trying to convince herself that hypnotic regression really was a good idea.

Gabe's gut clenched. If she wasn't sure, he sure as hell didn't want to put himself through it. "Have you changed your mind?" he asked, his voice coming out harder and more impatient than he'd intended.

"No," she said quickly. "I just hadn't anticipated starting this morning."

Gabe forced himself not to grab at the open excuse for delay. "Is that a problem? You said you didn't have to be at work until eleven."

Alicia's expression shifted, her features softening as if she'd just come to some sort of realization. "I can do it. But first, I'm going to take a shower and fix us some breakfast." Her lips curved in a smile that brightened her whole face. "I believe I promised you an omelet."

He couldn't muster a smile in return. "I'm not that hungry."

"Well, at least take a shower. Do you have a change of clothes with you?"

"I have something out in the truck," he said. "I'll go get it while you're showering." His gaze wandered over her body again, before he could stop himself. For an electric second, he could picture her, as clear as a photograph, naked and slick beneath the spray of the shower.

Her eyes darkened to coal as she returned his gaze. Her voice escaped in a soft rasp. "Okay, you do that." She backed out of the living room and disappeared into the hallway.

Gabe slumped back against the door. What the hell was he doing? She was eight years his junior, off-limits for about a thousand different reasons and he should have his mind on murders, not a naked grad student.

He forced himself out to his truck for a change of clothes, taking his own sweet time in hopes that the next time he saw Alicia Solano, she'd be fully dressed.

WHILE GABE SHOWERED AND CHANGED into fresh clothes, Alicia distracted herself by preparing a breakfast omelet, searching the recesses of her refrigerator for peppers and onions that hadn't gone bad due to her neglect. She found a red pepper that didn't look too wilted and half an onion that still seemed firm. Declaring victory, she grabbed the carton of eggs from the refrigerator door and headed for the stove.

She was flipping the omelet onto a large plate when Gabe came into the kitchen, smelling like herbal shower gel and pear shampoo. Somehow he made the fragrance seem masculine. He had changed into a fresh pair of jeans and a charcoal gray T-shirt that hugged the contours of his broad chest.

"Need any help?" he asked, leaning against the kitchen counter and watching her work. The charcoal shirt had turned his blue eyes smoky, as if something were smoldering deep inside him. She felt an answering flame flickering low in her belly.

She cleared the lump from her throat. "Maybe pour some orange juice? The glasses are in the cabinet over the toaster."

Gabe retrieved the glasses and opened the refrigerator to find the orange juice. While she divided the omelet, giving him the larger portion, he poured juice for them both.

Toast popped up in the toaster, warm and fragrant. She spread margarine on each slice and laid a piece on each plate.

"This is very good," Gabe pronounced a few minutes later, after sampling the omelet.

"Anyone can make a good omelet," she said, a little appalled at how much his praise pleased her. She could imagine her mother's look of disapproval—cooking for a man!

"Do you like to cook?"

"I'm not very practiced at it," she admitted. "My mom thought cooking was a sign of male oppression, so she never did any cooking herself. She just hired a live-in cook and housekeeper."

Gabe's eyebrows twitched. "A woman?"

Alicia smiled ruefully. "Of course. Anita Gonzales. Made the best fish tacos I've ever tasted."

"Are your parents wealthy?"

"I suppose so, although they'd be appalled to hear themselves described that way." Alicia poked at her omelet, her appetite receding. The topic of her parents wasn't one she liked to discuss much, despite the obsessive interest some of her professors and fellow instructors had in her famous parents.

Nothing like being the offspring of infamous radical-chic professors to guarantee your place as the darling of the college faculty lounge.

"What about your family?" Alicia asked.

Gabe picked up his slice of toast and turned it between his fingers. "I guess we're reasonably well-off. Dad and Mom own their own business and half of us work for them in some capacity. We own our own boats and vehicles, our own homes—we're doing okay for ourselves."

"You're a professional fisherman, right?" She nibbled at her toast. "What does that entail?"

He smiled at her words. "It entails a lot of sitting in a boat, trying to teach people to do in one day what it's taken me a lifetime to learn how to do. Most of the time, I'm a fishing guide, you see."

"People pay you to take them fishing?"

"More or less. I know all the spawning areas, all the places where fish find cover, the way the weather and the seasons affect bass patterns—stuff you can't figure out on your own in a day or two. People pay me for what I know. I also fish tournaments now and then and sometimes win prize money. I don't do that as much now."

"I guess it's more work than it sounds like, huh?"

"No, I get to fish and make money doing it. It's about the best job in the world." He grinned at her. "I bet you've never been fishing."

She shook her head. "My parents are vegans."

He glanced down at the plate of eggs. "But you're not?"

"Tried a burger once, never could go back to tofu after that." She smiled. "Call me a rebel."

His soft laugh was the sexiest thing she'd ever heard. She had to clutch the edge of the table to keep from melting into a puddle on the floor.

"So, what do your parents do? College professors, too?"

His casual question managed to dash a little cold water on her internal heat wave. "Yeah, actually. They're both professors at UC Berkeley, in the Poli-Sci department."

Gabe's eyebrows twitched. "Oh. *Those* Solanos."

Her heart sank. He recognized the name now. Everyone did, eventually. Even if her parents hadn't been famous former radicals who were now friends with half of the Washington establishment, there were her brother Sinclair's exploits in South America to reckon with. Not many girls could boast both parents who could easily score a visit to a state dinner and a brother who'd spent five years on the FBI's Most Wanted list before he blew himself up in a botched terrorist attack.

"Sinclair Solano was your brother." Gabe's words were low and neutral, making it hard to guess what he was thinking.

Among her academic colleagues, for the most part, her radical connections gave her antiestablishment street cred, even though she had never been a big fan of her parents' political posturing and certainly not her brother's crimes.

On the other hand, her relationship to one of the country's

most notorious homegrown radicals made it next to impossible to win the trust of the cops and other law enforcement officers she came into contact with as part of her studies.

"Yes," she admitted aloud, waiting for his response. If she had to make a prediction, she'd go with mistrust. After all, hadn't he said he was a part-time deputy?

He just nodded. "That had to hurt, losing him that way."

She shot another look his way, trying to read his thoughts. "It was bad," she said carefully.

"It can be tough to love someone who lets you down. Even harder to lose them in the middle of all that. Maybe hurts worse that way."

She stared at him openly now, surprised by how he really seemed to understand how she'd felt. "I did love him. I wanted him to stop what he was doing."

"You can't love someone into doing the right thing. It would be nice if that worked, but it doesn't."

"My parents couldn't decide if they were embarrassed by him or proud of him," she blurted, her tone more bitter than she had intended. "He took things so much farther than they did—their radicalism never quite reached the 'plant a bomb' stage. But they believed in the cause, even if they didn't approve his methods. Sometimes I wonder if they wished they'd had the guts to go as far as Sin did——" She clamped her mouth shut quickly, horrified at how much of her own anger and hurt she'd revealed to a virtual stranger. "I'm sorry. This isn't something I should be subjecting you to."

"We all have our family issues."

She shot him a skeptical look. "Yeah? What's the Cooper family secret?"

He smiled faintly. "If I told, it wouldn't be a secret."

Before she could protest, a trilling sound interrupted.

Gabe shifted in his seat, pulling his cell phone from the pocket of his jeans. "It's Cissy," he murmured before he answered. "Hey, kiddo. What's up?"

His gaze slanted toward Alicia, and he lowered his voice. "Yeah, that's my truck parked outside."

Well, hell, Alicia thought, wincing a little. She wasn't a prude—God knew, you couldn't grow up a prude in the Solano household—but she certainly didn't do sleepovers on the first date, much less the first meeting. At least Cissy wasn't a gossip. She just hoped Marlon was equally discreet.

"Yeah, it has to do with the cases," Gabe admitted. After a pause, he quickly added, "No, don't do…that." With a sigh, Gabe flipped his phone shut. "Cissy's on her way over."

"Are you going to tell her about the new murder?"

He nodded. "She'll read about it anyway. She's smart enough to put two and two together."

A knock on the door drew Alicia to her feet. She let Cissy into the apartment.

"What's happened?" Cissy asked.

Alicia looked at Gabe. He crossed to his niece's side and put his hand on her shoulder. "There's been another murder."

Cissy's brow wrinkled. "When?"

"Last night, a little before eleven. I found the body."

The horrified look on Cissy's face made Alicia's stomach knot. "Oh, Uncle Gabe—again?"

He squeezed her shoulder. "I stopped at a convenience store to stock up on a few snacks, since I didn't eat much at dinner. When nobody came to ring me up, I went looking for the clerk. I found her in a back room."

Cissy looked at Alicia. "Same signature?"

"We think so," she told the younger woman.

"So, three in the last five months." Cissy's tone of voice went grim. "Are they escalating?"

"Hard to say," Alicia admitted. "We don't know how many murders we still haven't connected to the killers."

"You should have called me last night," Cissy told Gabe. "Why didn't you?"

"It was late. I didn't want to wake you."

"But you didn't have a problem waking Alicia?" Cissy looked at Alicia. "What aren't y'all telling me?"

"What do you mean?" Alicia asked.

"Look, I know the two of you well enough to know you didn't just hook up for the night, which means Uncle Gabe came here and stayed here for a reason." Cissy's green eyes darkened. "Are you in danger, Alicia? We've never really talked about it, but you do fit the profile—"

"That's not why Gabe stayed," Alicia said firmly.

"Then why?"

Alicia looked at Gabe. Reluctance colored his expression, but when he spoke, he got right to the point. "I've asked Alicia to hypnotize me to see if I can remember anything about the night your mother died."

Cissy's puzzled expression cleared. "Good. When do we get started?"

"*We* don't," he answered firmly.

Cissy frowned. "She was my mother. I have a right to sit in on this."

"I don't want you to," Gabe replied.

Cissy turned to Alicia. "Tell him it's okay."

"It's his decision," Alicia answered. "Technically, he'll be my patient, at least during the duration of the hypnosis."

"That is such bull!" Cissy turned to her uncle. "You're trying to protect me. You're treating me like I'm still a little kid."

"Damned right I'm trying to protect you," Gabe answered

hotly. "And it has nothing to do with your age. I wouldn't want your daddy sitting in on this, either. Would you want your daddy to have to relive that night, in extra detail?"

Moisture welled in Cissy's eyes. "No."

"Then don't ask me to subject you to it, either." Gabe looked at her, pleading in his smoky blue eyes.

Cissy's tears spilled, but she lifted her chin. "Okay. I should probably go to class this morning anyway. Can't get by on my good looks and personality forever."

Gabe cupped her cheek. "Yeah, that Cooper charm will only go so far."

She wrapped her arms around her uncle's waist, pressing her cheek to his shoulder. Gabe hugged her close, placing a gentle kiss on top of her head. "I'll let you know anything new we learn," he promised.

He walked her to the door, promising a second time to call her later to let her know what happened. He closed the door behind her, leaning heavily against the solid wood panel with his eyes closed for a long moment before opening his eyes to meet Alicia's gaze.

"Are you ready to do this?" he asked.

She cocked her head. "Are you?"

He took a deep breath and let it out slowly. "Yeah. I'm ready. Let's do this."

Her heart starting to gallop with trepidation, Alicia went to her room to get what she needed.

Chapter Six

A metronome ticked a slow, steady rhythm on the coffee table that now sat a little to the side of the sofa. Alicia had said the beat would help him relax. He supposed it was a way to occupy his mind and keep it from getting in the way of the hypnosis. He wasn't sure it would work, however. He didn't think he'd ever relax again.

Alicia sat on the ottoman across from him, so close that her knees almost touched his. She'd moved the coffee table aside so that nothing would separate them during the session. Gabe found the warmth emanating from her body comforting, somehow. He was tempted to open his eyes, just to reassure himself that she was really there. But she'd asked him to close his eyes and shut out everything but her voice, so he squelched the urge and concentrated on listening to her steady breathing.

"Before we get started, let's talk about how you can control things when you're under."

"Control things?"

"We're going to go places that you'll find uncomfortable. It'll be easier for you to take chances if you know you can escape somewhere safe any time you want to."

He frowned slightly. This whole hypnosis idea sounded like nothing but hokum. But he knew his sister Hannah had found hypnosis helpful a couple of years ago, when she was trying to push through lingering amnesia about an attack that had nearly taken her life. She was a sensible, pragmatic woman. If it had worked for her, maybe it would work for him, too.

"Where do you feel safest, Gabe?"

"My boat," he answered without thinking.

Alicia went quiet for a moment. He gave into temptation and opened his eyes. She was struggling against a smile.

"You find that funny?" he asked, amused by her amusement.

She got the smile under control. "No. If your boat makes you feel safe—"

"You want to ask why, don't you?"

"It's not my place to question—"

"I know who I am when I'm in the boat. I know every inch of her. What makes her go. What makes her stop. I know how to guide her to places almost nobody else in the world knows about on the lake. I know how to ease her into a slip without even brushing against the dock."

"You're in complete control?"

He nodded, closing his eyes again. "Yes."

Her voice softened. "That's a good safe place. When it gets too crazy, you get in your boat and drive wherever you want. In fact, let's go there now. Imagine you're in the boat. What are you doing?"

An image flashed into his head—a wooded cove on Lake Gossamer where he sometimes went when he was fishing alone, just for his own pleasure. The water was shallow there, and clear enough to see the round spawning beds of the fat little bluegills he was fishing for. A light breeze rippled the water, bringing with it the faint, watermelon-like scent of bluegills on their beds.

"I'm fishing," he answered. "It's warm with a little breeze, and the bluegills are on their beds."

"Can you sit down in your boat?"

He felt the vinyl seat beneath him. "Yes."

"Good. I want you to sit down and let all the tension leave your legs."

He tried to do as she asked, focusing his mind on making his legs feel weightless and limp.

Alicia's warm words bathed him in serenity. "The seat will take all your weight. You want to let it hold you up. Stop fighting—just let the seat take all your weight."

The fishing seat on the prow of his boat seemed to grow larger, stronger, enveloping his legs until he could barely feel anything but the softness swaddling his limbs.

But the knot in his gut was as tight as ever.

"That's good," Alicia murmured. "Are you ready to leave the boat now and go take a trip to the past?"

His chest tightened. "I'm not sure."

"We don't have to go straight there. We can go somewhere else for a bit. A happier place and time. What were you doing that night before you went to the trucking company?"

He was suddenly in a hot, loud bar in Borland, a town just across the county line. Chickasaw County was a dry county, but you could get a beer over in Borland. That's where his friend Cam had wanted to meet his old high school buddies for an impromptu reunion during his brief trip back to town before he headed to New York to start his Wall Street job.

"I went to a bar," he answered. "A place called Lucky's. Cheap beer, pretty girls, a couple of pool tables and nobody calling the cops if you make a bet or two."

"Were you alone?"

He shook his head, surprised by how loose the muscles of his neck felt. "A friend from high school was home for a couple of days. He'd just graduated from Texas and was heading to a brokerage firm in New York. All the guys got together to give him a little send-off."

"You were glad to see him?"

"Yeah." Gabe smiled. "It was strange. In a lot of ways, he was the same old Cam. But I also knew I'd probably never see him again, once he went to New York. So I felt sad at the same time. For myself, I guess. I knew my life had changed and would never be what it was before."

"Were you drinking?"

"A beer. I wasn't drunk." He heard the defensive tone in his voice but felt oddly detached from the emotion behind it. It was like listening to someone else speak.

"When did you leave the bar?"

The big, round clock on the bar wall flashed in his head, the hands on the eleven and the five, filling him with dread. "I realized it was after eleven, and that's when Brenda got off work. I was twenty minutes away. I knew I was gonna be late."

"What time did you get to the trucking company office?"

He struggled to remember. He'd looked at the clock on the dashboard, hadn't he? What time had it been?

He saw the glowing light change from 11:22 p.m. to 11:23 p.m. "11:23 p.m.," he answered grimly. *Too late.*

"Tell me about the trucking company office. Was it on a main highway?"

"No. It was off the highway, on Piedmont Road."

"Was there anyone else around? Do you remember passing anyone on Piedmont Road?"

"No. Piedmont dead-ends at the trucking company. I'd have remembered—" The sudden image of bright lights made him wince. "Wait. There wasn't anyone on Piedmont, but just before I got there, I passed another car coming the opposite direction. They had their high beams on. Nearly blinded me."

"Could the car have turned onto the highway from Piedmont?"

"I don't know. Maybe." He'd rounded a curve and the car had just been there. It could have been on the highway already or it could have just turned onto the highway from Piedmont or any of the other side roads in that area.

"Do you remember anything about the car you passed?"

Gabe crinkled his brow, trying to picture the vehicle. That stretch of the highway didn't have lamps to illuminate the roadway. He'd caught a quick glimpse of the other car as it passed, lit by the headlights of his old Jeep. Distinguishing color in the low light was next to impossible, but had he seen more than he remembered? "I'm not sure—"

"Why don't we try slowing things down? Imagine you're in a movie, and the scene is playing out in slow motion. Everything winds down." Alicia's voice slowed as well, going low and fluid, as if she'd entered the slow motion scene with him.

He saw himself rounding the curve. The headlights coming down the highway shimmered into view, and for a second, they were all he could see. He slowed the scene down in his mind, until everything seemed to freeze in place.

"It's a sedan, I think," he murmured, taking in the oblong shape of the headlights.

"That's good." Alicia's voice seemed closer. He could smell her, too, the sweet, heady scent of honeysuckle on the vine. He wanted to open his eyes and see if she looked as good as she smelled, but his eyelids felt leaden, unable to move.

He dragged his mind back to the scene spread out before

him like a still life. The car beside him was dark—blue or black, perhaps. He counted the door handles—two, which meant it was a four-door. The windows were tinted, making it hard to see inside, but there was a light glow from within, as if there were a dashboard light on. He could make out the driver's silhouette. And there was someone in the passenger seat.

Excitement rippled through his chest, bubbling in his throat. "It's a four-door sedan. And there were two people in the vehicle. The driver and someone in the passenger seat."

"Did you see their faces?"

"No. I'm sorry. Tinted windows."

"That's okay, you're doing great."

"I can't tell the model of the car, but I think it's an Oldsmobile. From the shape," he added. The freeze-frame in his mind released, and the sudden resumption of movement made him feel off-kilter. He clutched at the sofa cushion beneath his hands to regain his balance.

"That's wonderful. You're doing so well."

The flicker of pleasure her praise elicited faded into growing dread. "I have to keep going, don't I?"

"Just a little further," she confirmed, sympathy softening her words. "Do you want to take a rest? We can go back to the boat for a while."

He was tempted to say yes, to go back to his safe place, just to regroup. But he was afraid if he retreated now, he wouldn't find the courage to go back to the place where the whole nightmare had begun.

"No. Let's keep going."

He felt the lightest brush of fingertips across the back of his right hand. "Okay," Alicia said. "Are you ready?"

"I'm turning off the highway onto Piedmont Road." He forced himself forward, trying to memorize every detail of his surroundings. The leaves were almost gone from the trees flanking the road, rendering them dark skeletons stretching thousands of bony black fingers skyward toward the waxing moon.

The skin on the back of his neck crawled relentlessly.

Ahead, Belmont Trucking Company sprawled, its dingy gray facade silent and still. There was no life there, Gabe knew, his pulse hammering in his temples.

No life at all.

"Can you see anyone around?"

He forced his gaze to scan the landscape of his memory. There was no sign of movement. Nothing out of place.

Nothing but the nightmare he knew lay just ahead, waiting for his discovery.

"No," he said. "There's no one else here."

He felt her hand on his again. Her touch was firm this time. Firm and warm.

"Let's go back to the boat," she said.

He turned his hand over, catching hers. Her soft palm settled into the cradle of his own. He closed his fingers around her hand, not ready to release her.

Letting go of the darkness, he returned to the boat.

Blinding light filled his mind, clean and sweet, its heat driving away the memory of the November chill. The rippling water around him glittered with sunlit diamonds, rocking the boat like a cradle.

Standing close enough to touch, in a fluttery white dress that showed off her delicious curves, Alicia smiled at him. The breeze over the water tousled her hair, driving tendrils around his own head until he felt ensnared by her.

"I'm in the boat," he murmured, his heart pounding. "Can we stay here a little while?"

Her hand flexed against his, her thumb sliding gently

across the side of his hand. "We can stay as long as you need."

He smiled faintly. "I don't know about that—I can stay on the water all day." *Especially with you standing so near, smelling like summer honeysuckle.*

"Well, we can stay another hour until I have to go to work," she amended, her voice light with humor.

With a sigh, he left the boat behind and opened his eyes. Alicia was closer than he expected, her hand still clasped in his. Her dark eyes met his, wide and liquid.

The urge to kiss her swamped him, stealing his breath.

Those dark eyes widened suddenly, as if she'd read his intent in his blistering gaze. She tugged her hand away and rose from the ottoman, her gait unsteady as she made her way toward the kitchen.

"Can I get you a glass of water?" she asked.

"No, I'm okay." He dragged his gaze away from her curvy backside and concentrated on remembering the details of his recent foray into his subconscious. "A four-door Olds. Do you think it could be connected?"

"Well, at the very least, maybe we can figure out a way to track down Victor Logan's driving history. If he ever owned an Oldsmobile, we may be on to something." Alicia sipped the glass of water she'd poured for herself, remaining at a safe distance, her back pressed against the kitchen counter.

"I wish I'd remembered more."

"You did great. Seriously. Hypnosis is pretty hit and miss, and you cooperated every step of the way."

Maybe a little too much, he thought, remembering his last vision of her on the boat. He needed to get out of here, at least for a little while. Go back to the motel, get something to eat. Maybe make a few calls back home, see how things were going at the marina.

Anything to ground himself in his life away from here. Away from her.

He pushed to his feet. "Listen, I need to get out of your hair for a while. I know you need to get ready for work and I should touch base back home and see what's going on at the office. Make sure they'll be okay if I stay here another day."

"Oh." Alicia set her glass on the counter. "Okay, that's a good idea. So you're thinking of staying another day?"

There was a small voice in the back of his head yelling at him to get the hell out of Millbridge. He had a life back home in Gossamer Ridge. A job he loved. A family who needed him almost as much as he needed them.

A life that was settled and uncomplicated.

"Yeah," he answered, ignoring the voice. "At least another day or two. The police may have more questions for me about last night's murder."

And I may have more questions for you about your research into Brenda's murder, he added silently.

"Probably," she agreed, returning to the living room. "You're sure you're not a suspect? Because if you need someone to go to bat for you—"

"I'm not a suspect," he assured her. "I told you, I had them call my brother Aaron, who's a sheriff's deputy. He convinced the officers I'm an upright, tax-paying citizen. Cops seem to listen to other cops."

"Good." She was close enough to touch again and Gabe felt his fingers itching to reach out and pull her closer.

He forced his reluctant feet toward the door. "I really appreciate your offer of the sofa last night."

"No problem," she said with a smile that carved a pretty dimple in her cheek. She followed him to the door, gazing up at him as she opened it for him. But if he hoped to read her mind in that liquid gaze, he was thwarted. Whatever thoughts and emotions writhed beneath the surface were unfathomable, hidden in the depths of her dark eyes.

He stepped outside into the pleasant May morning, wincing a little as the door closed behind him. When he reached his truck parked on the curb, he was only slightly surprised to find his niece sitting on the bumper, waiting for him.

"I thought you had a class this morning."

Cissy glanced at her watch. "Not for another thirty minutes."

Gabe hit the lock tab on his keychain, disengaging the truck's locks. "Get in. I'll drive you."

Cissy settled into the passenger seat, buckling in while Gabe slid behind the steering wheel. "How did it go?"

"Okay."

"Did you remember anything new?"

He didn't want to get her hopes up. "I'm not sure. I remembered seeing a car on the highway just before the turnoff to the trucking company where your mama worked. But I can't say for sure the car was related to what happened."

"But it could be," she pressed.

"Maybe."

Cissy fell silent a moment while he put the truck in gear and edged out onto the street. They reached the intersection ahead and Gabe turned right, heading toward the university.

"Are you heading back home now?" she asked as they neared the campus.

"No, I'm going to stick around another day or two."

She released a soft breath. "So you think Alicia's onto something? With her theory?"

A memory flashed in his head—the darkened sedan, with two occupants in the front seats. "I think it's possible."

But did the new knowledge get them any closer to catching the killers?

Chapter Seven

For the most part, Alicia's classes were fun if not particularly challenging to teach. She handled a couple of first year psychology courses that the college required all students to take, and most of the students were there because they had to be, not because they were really interested in psychology. But Alicia saw their apathy as a challenge, taking pride in coaxing real interest out of all her students.

Other students took to the courses right away, digging into the subject matter with a real intellectual hunger that made her understand a little better her own parents' passion for their careers as professors. Alicia herself didn't have plans to stay in academia; she'd been thinking of applying to the FBI or the Diplomatic Security Service once she had her doctorate. But she finally understood the appeal of teaching after all these years of swearing she'd never turn into her parents.

Her busy course schedule gave her little time to think about the new murder—or about Gabe Cooper and what he might be doing with his day. But when she headed back to her tiny office after her last class concluded at three, her thoughts returned to Gabe and their hypnosis session that morning. She couldn't be sure his memory of the second vehicle had anything to do with the murders, but a little hope never hurt anyone. So she hoped like hell that Tony would call her with news that Victor Logan had once owned and driven a four-door Oldsmobile.

She wondered if Gabe Cooper was serious about sticking around Millbridge for another day or two. He had work he was neglecting in Gossamer Ridge, and it wasn't like he couldn't follow the Millbridge cases from across the state, especially since he had a brother who was a cop.

Maybe he'd decided to leave, after all. Maybe she'd get home to find a message on her answering machine, saying good-bye.

Or maybe he'd just leave without telling her anything at all. It wasn't like he owed her anything, was it?

She pushed her sweat-damp hair away from her forehead, irritated. The air conditioning in the behavioral sciences building was temperamental and, in her opinion, vindictive, choosing the warmest days of the year to be at its most uncooperative. The air coming from the vent by her desk was tepid at best. With unseasonably warm temperatures soaring to the mid-nineties, tepid wasn't good enough.

She needed a shower. A nice, cool shower, a glass of ice water and maybe an early dinner of fresh fruit and cheese. She had another hour's worth of paperwork to do, which she normally tried to handle here at the office so she could devote her time at home to her dissertation. But she couldn't bear another hour stuck in this cluttered little sauna. She packed the papers into her briefcase and headed for home.

With the sun still high in the sky, the tree-lined streets held no threat of danger, only scenic pleasure. She was almost to the corner of University Drive and Dogwood Street when she heard someone call her name.

Turning, she saw one of her students, Tyler Landon, approaching at a fast pace. "Alicia, wait up."

She frowned at his easy use of her first name. In class,

she maintained control by adhering to formal address. She was Ms. Solano. She addressed the students in kind—Ms. Cooper, Mr. Landon—to maintain that formality.

Of course, Tyler Landon was only three years younger than she was, having started college late after spending a few years traveling. She supposed, since they weren't in the classroom, Tyler Landon might find it easier to address her as an equal.

"Can I help you with something?" she asked as he drew near.

"Just wondering why you were headed home so early. You usually stay later than this, you know, working on your papers and all."

Tyler had a lazy drawl and a pair of bright blue eyes that she supposed more than a few young coeds would describe as dreamy. But neither attribute did anything for Alicia, proving that she wasn't susceptible to *all* good-looking Southern men.

Especially not young men who seemed to harbor an inappropriate amount of interest in what she did with her time.

"It was hot in the office, so I thought I'd take my work home," she answered simply.

"Oh, so you live near here?"

The tree-lined street no longer seemed so free of danger. "Was there a particular reason you flagged me down?" she asked, erasing her smile. She didn't want him to get any wrong ideas about the nature of their relationship.

"I heard there was another one of those murders," Tyler said, cocking his head to one side. "I hear you're doing some paper on them. I wondered if you could use some help."

She couldn't decide whether or not it was safe to relax

her guard. After all, this wasn't the first time a student had expressed interest in her work. To some kids, murder investigations probably seemed exciting, even glamorous.

Of course, that perception rarely lasted past their first face-to-face encounter with a dead body.

"I appreciate the offer, Tyler, but I have to do the work on my own. You understand."

"I know you talk to the police. You get help from them, don't you?" Tyler took a couple of steps forward, brushing his sandy hair out of his face. "Like that cop you were seeing. You're not still seeing him, are you?"

Alarm it is, she thought. "Tyler, my personal life isn't an appropriate topic of conversation between us. Do you understand that?"

His mouth flattened with annoyance. "You're not that much older than I am. Hardly at all."

"I'm your teacher. Age is irrelevant." As he looked ready to argue, she quickly added, "I have to go. I have plans to meet a friend for dinner." She started to walk away.

"A date?" he asked.

She swung around to face him. "None of your business."

He held up his hands as if in defeat. "God, you feminist types can be real bitches."

She bit back a retort, knowing that arguing with him would only escalate the situation. Instead, she turned and walked away, deliberately passing her street and walking on, not wanting him to know where she lived.

She circled the block and came in from the other end of the street, scanning the area carefully to make sure Tyler hadn't followed her. Ahead, her apartment building slumbered like an elegant old lady, a little worn by time but still retaining the essence of beauty she must have possessed in her youth. Alicia felt a surprising surge of affection for the place as she climbed the steps and headed for her front door, keys in hand.

She stopped short in front of the faded welcome mat, spotting a white, letter-sized envelope propped against the front door. Her name was printed in block letters on the front.

She looked around quickly, the hair on her arms standing on end. Did Tyler know where she lived, after all?

Seeing no one watching her, Alicia crouched and picked up the envelope. There was nothing on it but her name.

With a sinking sensation in her belly that she didn't want to think about too closely, she slid her finger under the flap of the envelope, certain it was a quick goodbye note from Gabe Cooper. She'd pushed him too hard that morning, forced him to delve into areas of his mind he wasn't ready to examine.

Or worse, had he sensed her attraction to him and decided to nip things in the bud before she embarrassed herself further? She didn't know whether to feel humiliated or relieved.

The envelope came open and all thoughts of Gabe Cooper fled when she pulled out the contents, a single three-by-five index card. On the lined side were three words, written in the same heavy block lettering as her name on the front.

"You are 22," she read aloud, her brow creasing.

She flipped the card over to see if there was anything else written on the card. It was otherwise blank.

She rose to her feet, puzzling over the note. She was 22? What the hell did that mean?

Her cell phone rang, making her jump. She slid the card back in the envelope and pulled her phone from the side pocket of her briefcase. "Hello?"

"Alicia, it's Gabe Cooper. I'm at last night's crime scene and I think I found something strange. How soon can you get here?"

ALICIA SOLANO'S SMALL FORD Focus pulled into the abandoned parking lot across the street from the convenience store and parked beside Gabe's truck. He got out to greet her, noting that unlike yesterday, she was dressed in a form-fitting yellow sundress that showed off her toned arms and shapely legs. The color emphasized the honey tones of her skin and the hair spilling around her shoulders in thick, dark waves.

"You said you found something strange?" She didn't bother with a greeting, just crossed to his side in a couple of purposeful strides. "Why did you come back here?"

"To see if I could remember anything I might have overlooked the night I found the body."

Now that she was here, he was beginning to doubt his own motives. What he found might be interesting. It could also be nothing. Had he just called her up and lured her here to give him an excuse to see her again?

"It could be nothing," he said, gesturing for her to walk with him across the street, to where yellow caution tape blocked off the store and parking lot.

He led her around to the side of the convenience store building, which consisted of a plain brick wall. It was completely blank, except for a large black "21" spray painted onto the bricks near the back of the building.

Alicia let out a soft gasp.

Gabe turned to look at her, surprised to find her staring at the wall with alarm. Her face seemed pale beneath her golden tan and she turned her dark eyes to his.

"What is it?"

She looked back at the wall. "Twenty-one."

He nodded. "Does that mean anything?"

"Do you have a handkerchief? Or maybe a napkin?"

He didn't have a handkerchief, but he'd gone to a drive-through restaurant for lunch and there should be some left-over napkins in the bag on his passenger seat. He fetched one and returned to her. "What's going on?"

She took the napkin and reached into her pocket, pulling out a white envelope with her name printed on it in blocky black letters. She handed it to Gabe, taking care to hold the napkin in place. "Use the napkin to hold it. I may have already ruined any chance of getting prints off it, but—"

He took the envelope, tearing the napkin in two pieces so he could open it without letting his fingers touch the paper. Inside, he found a small index card. On the card, the words "You are 22" were written in the same handwriting.

"Damn," he said aloud.

"It has to be connected, don't you think?" She looked at him, her expression tinged with hope that he'd contradict her.

"I don't know."

"Can we be sure that's fresh paint?"

"It is. I went under the caution tape to check. It's dry on the wall, but some of it dripped down onto some trash on the ground, including a register tape dated yesterday evening around eight o'clock." Seeing the look of fear in her eyes, he wished he could have given her a different answer. "I didn't touch it. Just looked at it. I think maybe you should call your friend in the police department. This could be important."

"I don't remember anything like this at the other murder scenes." Alicia's voice came out in a raspy half-whisper. She was hugging her arms as if she were cold, although it was as hot as hell out here in the full sun.

He cupped her elbow, feeling her arm tremble at his

touch. "Why don't you go on back to your place? I'll call the cops, tell them what I found."

"No, I'll call them." She lifted her chin. "You should go. They might be wondering why you came back to the crime scene. Don't want them putting you back on the suspect list."

He gestured with the envelope he still held. "This could very well mean you're a target. I'm not leaving here without you. No way."

She looked at him, her eyes wide and dark. "I have a friend who's a police officer. I'll call him. He'll know the best way to handle this." She pulled her phone from the pocket of her sundress and dialed a number. A moment later, she said, "Hi, Tony, it's Alicia."

She seemed to know this Tony person well, her tone friendly and, on occasion, almost intimate. She'd mentioned she used to date a cop. He guessed this Tony must be the guy.

Alicia hung up the phone. "Tony's on the way. He's not actually investigating this case, but I already convinced him to look into Victor Logan's driving history, so he sort of has a vested interest."

"Is Tony the ex-boyfriend?" Gabe kept his voice light.

Alicia shot him an odd look. "I told you about him?"

"I think you said he helped you get access to files and other material."

"Right." Her eyes strayed back to the spray painting on the brick wall of the convenience store.

"How long were you together?"

"Only four months. Our schedules didn't mesh—his work, my work. I guess we just didn't really want the relationship enough to make it work."

He'd had a few relationships like that. Most of his relationships had been like that, really. Women had trouble understanding why he'd drop everything to go on another wild goose chase to find out who killed his sister-in-law.

He'd canceled his share of dates and getaway weekends over the years when another lead cropped up unexpectedly. None of his girlfriends had ever really understood his stake in the investigation.

Of course, he'd never told any of them the truth about his own terrible connection to the murder, had he? He'd been too ashamed, too guilty about his mistakes to share the truth with any of the women he'd dated over the past decade. Maybe if he had, one of them would have understood what drove him and supported his decisions instead of walking away.

But he'd never told anyone. Not because he didn't think they'd understand and maybe even support him.

He was beginning to suspect it was because he was afraid they would. He was afraid one of them would hear the whole story and try to convince him he was being too hard on himself. And maybe, if he'd heard it enough, he might start to believe.

He couldn't do that. His brother had spent the last twelve years without the love of his life. He had a lifetime of grief and loss ahead of him because of what Gabe had done. Cissy and her brother Mike had lived most of their lives without their mother and they'd spend the rest of their lives without her.

How could he bear even a hint of happiness when he'd brought such loss to people he loved so much?

"I've found only fifteen murders I thought were connected," Alicia murmured, drawing his thoughts back to their more pressing problem. "I thought I was thorough. But if these numbers mean what I think they mean—"

"Why now?" Gabe asked. "There was no number left at Brenda's crime scene. And as thorough as you seem to have been, I would think you'd have noticed if other numbers had been left at other crime scenes."

"I went to the other two crime scenes—one five days afterwards, then the very next morning on the second one, once I realized they were probably connected." Alicia leaned against the side of Gabe's truck, rubbing her temples with her fingertips. "There was nothing like this at those scenes."

"So why now?" he repeated. "That note—it was a message to you. It had your name on it."

"Whoever's doing this knows I'm investigating the murders," Alicia said flatly. "They've decided I'm their next target."

"So why warn you?"

She shook her head. "It's a game? They want to show me they're smarter than me—so smart they can give me a warning and still defeat me?"

Gabe's chest tightened with anger. If those sons of bitches thought he was going to let them get to this woman, they'd badly overestimated their power. "Well, that's not going to happen. You're not alone like those other women. You're not going to be alone."

"I live alone. I walk to work and back every day, alone—"

"No more of that. You drive everywhere. No more walking alone." Gabe crossed to where she leaned against the truck, putting his hand on her shoulder. "And no living alone, either. I know you've got neighbors all around you, but that note proves the killers think they can get to you regardless. So you're not living alone, either."

"So, what—I get myself a roommate and now she's in danger, too?" Alicia shook her head firmly. "I'm not putting another woman in danger."

"Not a woman." Gabe leaned toward her. "Me."

Her eyes widened slightly. "You?"

"I've got enough money in savings to pay my bills for a couple of months. I don't have to go back home until we fix this." Even as he fleshed out his impromptu offer, Gabe realized just what he was offering. He was putting himself on the line between Alicia and at least one of the men who'd killed his sister-in-law.

And how had that worked out the last time?

"I can't ask you to do that," Alicia protested.

"You didn't ask." Gabe pushed away his doubts. What other choice did he have? Walk away and let her fight the monsters alone? That wasn't going to happen. "I'll sleep on the sofa. I'll drive you to work and pick you up when you're done."

"And what do you do in the interim—watch soaps and eat ice cream?" She gave him a skeptical look.

"I'll do a little investigating on my own," he replied. "I have training. I have a few police contacts of my own. And I've got nothing but time."

Her eyes narrowed as she contemplated his offer. "We share notes? No haring off on your own?"

He smiled at the suspicion in her voice. "If you'll promise the same."

She was silent for a moment. Then she nodded. "Okay."

Gabe released a pent up breath.

What the hell was he doing?

Chapter Eight

"You should be in protective custody." Tony Evans shot Alicia a sharp look as he returned from investigating the spray painting on the brick wall.

"I'll have protection." She slid a quick glance at Gabe, who had remained across the road in the abandoned parking lot where his truck and her Ford were parked. She'd crossed with Tony to show him the evidence that the crime scene technicians had missed.

"If this guy's targeting you—"

"These guys," she corrected, keeping her voice light to hide her growing sense of dread.

"Whatever." Tony didn't exactly buy into her theory of two killers working together. She didn't know why—such a situation wasn't unprecedented.

"You know serial killers sometimes work in pairs, Tony. Bianchi and Buono, the Copelands, Graham and Wood—"

"Yeah, but if *your* theory is right, one of these guys switches partners like a woman changes shoes."

"He changed partners once that we know of," she argued. "Victor Logan went to jail for running down Micah Davis, so he was out of commission for a few years. The alpha didn't have his beta partner anymore, so he found someone else."

"The younger guy." Tony had been the one who helped her get her hands on the statements of Jake Cooper and his wife Mariah, from the month before. They'd witnessed Victor Logan's death and had provided the tantalizing information that Logan had been cooperating with a younger, unidentified man shortly before his death.

Jake Cooper's wife, Mariah, who'd considered Victor Logan a mentor and a friend up until the time he killed her lover Micah, had been convinced that Victor was the man who'd killed Brenda Cooper. But Gabe's brother Jake wasn't as sure, pointing out that Victor's style of violence was more personal and indirect than a killer who found great pleasure in nearly gutting his victims with his own hand.

"I think it's possible the alpha's hooked up with a younger guy, yes."

Tony gave her a look that was somewhere between concern and exasperation. "You know most of the guys in the detective squad think you're a nut."

She lifted her chin. "What about you?"

"Oh, I've always thought you were a nut," he said with a grin. "But you're just so damned cute, I overlook it."

She lightly punched his arm. "Seriously."

"Seriously? I think you're probably onto something, and right now, it's scaring the hell out of me." He tugged a lock of her hair. "I know we're not together anymore and I'm totally on board with that—you were right that we'd never work together. But I still care and the thought of that guy—those guys—being after you full-bore—"

She caught his hand and gave it a squeeze. "I'll be careful. Gabe's going to play bodyguard—"

Tony's gaze wandered across the road to where Gabe stood beside his truck, his arms folded. He had been watching them the whole time; Alicia practically felt the weight of his gaze on her. "What do you know about this Cooper guy? Is he connected to Jake and Mariah Cooper?"

"He's Jake Cooper's brother."

"Which makes him the brother-in-law of Brenda Cooper," Tony added, glancing across the road. "He has his own stake in solving these murders. And that concerns me."

"Why?"

"What if his agenda clashes with yours? Is he going to put you at risk to get what he wants?"

Alicia looked across the road. Gabe seemed to be staring a hole through her. "He seems to be a man of his word. I believe him when he says he wants to help keep me safe while we investigate these cases."

"While we investigate?" Tony echoed. "He's playing private eye, too?"

"He's a deputy back in Chickasaw County," Alicia defended. But honesty compelled her to add. "Part-time auxiliary."

"Which basically means he's called in for manhunts, emergency search-and-rescue and the occasional natural disaster," Tony replied, his tone dismissive. "Great."

A surge of annoyance heated Alicia's face. "Oh, well I'll just have to tell him to go home now," she retorted. "Because protective custody in a fleabag motel with some geriatric Millbridge cop ogling me all night would be so much better."

"You'd rather be ogled by the tall, dark redneck all night?"

She slanted a look at Tony. "Go to hell."

He grinned. "You got a crush on Jethro Bodine?"

She turned without answering, crossing the road in a few angry strides.

Gabe pushed away from the truck to greet her. "Are you mad at him or me?"

She took a deep breath. "Neither." She heard the crunch of gravel behind her and realized Tony had followed her across the road. Pasting on a smile, she turned to face him. "So? What's the final verdict?"

Tony seemed a little thrown by her question, but he recovered quickly. "I think you're right. It does seem connected to the other Millbridge murders, at least. Same victim profile, same M.O., same signature. The spray paint is a new twist, but I don't think that negates the obvious similarities to the previous murders."

"I've been thinking about that," Gabe said, drawing Alicia's gaze back to him. "What if this is something more personal? Specific to Alicia, I mean."

"Specific how?" Tony asked.

"This is the first crime scene where the killer left a message. And then Alicia got the index card message this morning. It seems to me, both the spray paint and the card serve the same purpose—a message for Alicia."

"Because he knows I'm investigating the murders," Alicia replied, understanding his point.

"He wants you to be afraid," Tony said.

"I wish it were that simple." Gabe gave Alicia a troubled look. "But I think he meant what he wrote. He plans for her to be the next victim."

A cold flush shuddered through Alicia. She wrapped her arms more tightly around herself, barely feeling the pressing heat of the sun overhead.

"But why would he change his signature this way?" Tony asked. "Serial killers don't do that kind of thing. They kill a certain way, choose certain victims, because they satisfy whatever twisted need he has. He wouldn't just decide to pick a new victim out of irritation or a need to cover his tracks—"

"I fit the profile," Alicia murmured.

"It's not just that," Gabe added, reaching out to brush the side of Alicia's arm with his fingertips. "I've been thinking about it—why this would be different now. And I don't think it's the alpha who's leaving the messages."

Alicia looked up at him. "You think it's the beta?"

Gabe nodded. "I think he must know you. Personally."

"How?" Tony asked.

"Could be a student at the university or another faculty member. It could be someone in the maintenance crew." Gabe slanted a look at Tony. "Or a cop she's worked with."

Tony's lips flattened to a thin line, but he contained his irritation. "Clearly it's someone who knows she's been investigating these murders."

"That could be almost anyone," Alicia said, her chest tight with nervous tension. "I haven't exactly hidden my dissertation subject. All of my students would know and they might have told family or friends—" She stopped short, remembering her encounter with Tyler Landon that afternoon. "Oh, my God."

"What?" Gabe spoke, but both men looked up at her words.

"I had a really weird encounter with a student this afternoon, just before I found the note." She told them about her run-in with Tyler Landon. "I thought it was just an inappropriate student crush, but—"

"But it could be connected," Tony finished for her. "I'll run background on him, just to be sure."

"I don't want to believe it could be a student—" Alicia shook her head, feeling sick.

"You don't want to believe it could be anyone you know." Gabe laid a sympathetic hand on her arm.

"But what if it is?"

"Let's concentrate on keeping you safe first," Tony said firmly. "I can set up a safe house—"

"No." Alicia shook her head. "We discussed this."

Tony shot Gabe a considering look. "What qualifies you to protect her?"

Gabe returned the look, his expression deadly serious. "Do you remember hearing a news story last November about a shootout in Alabama involving a *Sanselmano* drug cartel?"

Tony gave him an odd look. "Sure. It was big news around these parts—we've had some trouble with the drug cartels ourselves. Story was, some ordinary family of fishermen—" He stopped short. "So. That was you."

Gabe nodded. "Well, my brothers, my sister-in-law, and me. And I'm not sure we really qualify as ordinary. My dad was a Marine Corps sniper in Vietnam. My brothers and sister and I have been shooting since we were old enough to hold a gun." He slanted a quick look at Alicia. "More to the point, I'm motivated."

Alicia studied his face, trying to read the exact meaning of his words. Motivated to keep her safe because she might be the key to solving Brenda's murder? Or because he had a personal reason for wanting to keep her alive?

Stop it. This is no time to go all girly.

She dragged her gaze back to Tony's face. He was watching her, his brow furrowed. Finally, he looked at Gabe, his expression clearing. "Okay, I guess you're qualified. But I want regular reports from both of you. And if anything gets really wiggy, don't play hero. We may not be a big, well-funded police force, but we do have a few tricks up our sleeves that civilians don't. And we can always call in the cavalry."

"Fair enough." Gabe gave a quick nod.

"I'm going to brief the detectives working the case. I'll

give them this." Tony held up a small plastic evidence bag containing the envelope and index card Alicia had found on her porch that afternoon. "They'll want to get a set of both your prints to eliminate."

"I didn't touch it with my fingers," Gabe said. "Just with a napkin."

"Just Alicia, then." Tony looked at her. "But they'll want to hear both of your statements, I'm sure."

"Aren't they going to wonder why Gabe was snooping around the crime scene? I don't want them to hare off on a theory that he's the real killer."

"Know what I'm wondering?" Tony gave Gabe a dark look, his hand hovering near his hip, where his service pistol nestled in its holster.

Alicia's heart skipped a beat. "Tony—"

His fingers settled over the holster snap. "How can you be so sure he's not the killer?"

Gabe didn't flinch, although Alicia noted he kept his eye on Tony's gun hand. "The police officers who responded to my 911 call last night checked me out for blood spatter and other trace evidence. They found nothing, of course." Gabe smiled, although the muscles in his jaw looked as hard as rocks. "Plus, my brother, the deputy, vouched for me. And I'm pretty sure I have solid alibis for the other murders, if you want to waste time checking them out."

Tony stared at him for a long moment, then dropped his hand away from the holster. He sighed, his gaze wandering back to the spray painting on the brick wall across the road. "Twenty-one murders?"

"Looks that way," Gabe answered.

"Well, hell…"

"I'm pretty sure those murders are spread out over at least a decade and three different states," Alicia said.

"Three?" Gabe asked. "I thought the murders were only

in Alabama and Mississippi. At least, that's all Mariah remembered from that scrapbook."

"What scrapbook?" Tony asked.

"Gabe's sister-in-law found a scrapbook Victor Logan was keeping—newspaper clippings about several similar murders. Remember, I told you about that."

"Right. But I thought that got burned up."

"It did, but Mariah saw it before that." Gabe's voice was tight with impatience. "Unfortunately, now it's stuck in the Mississippi state lab probably gathering dust unless they've miraculously figured out a way to restore any of those pages." He looked at Alicia. "What other state?"

"I've found one possible murder in Louisiana," she answered. "Outside New Orleans about seven years ago. But I can't be sure, because I haven't been able to confirm Victor Logan was in that area at the time, and he's the only suspect we've been able to identify so far."

Gabe frowned, as if the mention of New Orleans meant something to him. "Seven years ago? Do you remember what month?"

"October," she replied. "Does that mean something to you?"

"Maybe. I need to check on something." Gabe pulled out his cell phone and dialed a number.

He apparently had the phone on speaker, for a woman answered on the third ring, her voice tinny but understandable over the cell phone's speaker. "Hey, Gabe. Are you still in Millbridge?"

"Yeah, for another couple of days, at least." He slanted a quick look at Alicia. "Mariah, I'm on speakerphone. I'm here with a woman named Alicia Solano and a police officer named Tony Evans." He looked at Alicia and Tony. "This is Mariah, my brother Jake's wife. She's the one who knew Victor Logan."

"Gabe, what's going on?" Mariah's voice grew even tenser. "Why are we talking about Victor Logan?"

"Alicia's working on her doctoral dissertation. She's looking into Victor Logan's possible involvement in some old cold cases." He threw Alicia a warning look. Clearly, he didn't want to burden his sister-in-law with more information than what he'd already told her, so Alicia kept her clarifications to herself.

"Listen, when Victor Logan found you in New Orleans— do you remember exactly when that was?" Gabe asked.

"It's been seven years—let me think." Mariah's voice darkened, as if the last thing she wanted to do was think about the time she'd spent with Victor Logan.

Alicia couldn't blame her. But whether she liked it or not, Mariah Cooper was a material witness to those murders.

"It must have been October," Mariah answered finally. "I'm pretty sure I was panhandling at an Oktoberfest event. Some jerk had thrown a whole cup of beer on me and I reeked. Victor thought I was drunk at first."

"October, seven years ago." Gabe looked at Alicia. She gazed back at him, trying to keep a lid on her sudden surge of excitement. It might mean nothing.

But what were the odds that a similar murder would happen in New Orleans exactly the time Victor Logan had been there?

"Thanks, Mariah. That's what I needed to know. Give the family my love and I'll be in touch soon." Gabe hung up and looked at Alicia and Tony.

"So this Victor guy is looking pretty solid for the earlier murders," Tony said.

"He was the stalker. He found the victims. I don't think he actually killed them," Alicia said.

"He was the beta," Gabe said quietly.

She nodded. "I think whoever's acting as the beta now must be doing the same thing."

"And now he's stalking you." Tony sounded grim.

"Maybe that's a good thing," Alicia said, lifting her chin. But the way Gabe looked at her suggested she wasn't doing a good job of hiding her fear.

"How can it be a good thing?" Tony asked, answering fear in his voice. Their relationship might be over, but she knew he still cared about her.

"He made the mistake of letting me know he's stalking me," she answered. "He's getting overconfident, and that's going to come back to bite him."

"You hope," Tony muttered.

"Call the detectives in," Alicia said, setting aside any thoughts of her own situation. "Let's get this done."

After a long look at her, Tony stepped away and made the radio call to the station.

ALICIA STOOD OVER THE SINK in the ladies room at the Mill-bridge police station, scrubbing at the ink stains on her fingertips. She didn't know if there would be any other fingerprints to find on the index card—frankly, she doubted it, as the killers had been meticulous about leaving behind no evidence to implicate them in the murders. But the police were big on following procedure.

Once most of the ink was swirling down the drain, Alicia turned off the water and met her reflection in the mirror over the sink. She looked disheveled and terrified, her dark eyes wide and framed with dusky shadows.

Get a grip, Solano. You can't change anything. You can only make sure the perps don't get what they want.

Sometimes, it seemed as if the bulk of her life was completely out of her own control. From her parents, who reveled in their lives as flamboyant dilettantes, to her late brother, who'd gained his own notoriety through bullets and bombs, the Solano legacy was inescapable. People she met judged her by their reputation rather than her own actions, and nothing she did to separate herself from them seemed to make any difference at all.

Now, thanks to her own obsession with solving these serial murders, the killers had made her a target of their sick appetites—and she could do nothing but hide in her apartment and wait for them to make their moves.

How had she come to this point? What was she doing wrong?

A knock on the bathroom door made her jump.

"Alicia?" It was Gabe. He sounded worried.

"I'm coming," she called, reaching for the paper napkins on the wall. She dried her hands and crossed to the door.

Gabe stood on the other side, as if he'd been standing guard. Taking his job as her protector seriously already, she thought with amusement tinged with dismay.

"They said we can go. If they have any more questions, they'll call." Gabe laid his hand lightly on the small of her back, his touch warm and somehow bracing. It was all she could do not to lean in toward the solid heat of his body. "You want to stop somewhere and grab something for dinner?"

She didn't feel the least bit hungry. "I really should get back to the apartment. I brought a lot of work home with me."

"University stuff or your personal work?"

"Both, actually." They stopped at the property desk to retrieve the lethal-looking pistol Gabe had checked in upon entering the police station. He slipped it back into the holster at his waist and led her through the front door into the waning sunlight outside the police station, where their vehicles were parked in the visitor area.

"Are you sure you're okay? You look a little pale." Gabe stopped with her next to the driver's side door of her car. He lifted his hand to move a strand of hair away from her eyes. "Can't the work wait? You look like you need some food and a good night's sleep."

"You're my bodyguard, not my nanny," she retorted, careful to keep her tone light. She didn't want him to think she wasn't grateful for his help. But she didn't need mothering, either.

"Okay, fine." He dropped his hand away from her face. "But maybe I can help you out."

"Help me out?" She forced a smile. "What do you know about cognitive psychology?"

He returned her smile, though his eyes remained watchful. "About as much as you know about locating bass during a cold front. But I was talking about the murder cases. I could look over all your notes—you know, a fresh set of eyes. Might find something new."

"Something I've missed, you mean."

"Maybe. Or maybe with my experiences and background, I'll just find something that means more to me than it means to you." He eased the keys from her fingers and unlocked her car door. "I'll be right behind you. Don't get separated from me."

Part of her wanted to protest the way he expected her to follow his orders, but the rest of her was too tired and rattled to put up a fight. She led the way on the drive back to her apartment, taking care to stick to the more congested main roads rather than taking the shortcuts she'd normally use to cut the drive time by a third. They reached the apartment a little after five o'clock, parking in back-to-back slots at the curb.

Cissy Cooper sat on the wooden steps leading up to the apartment's wraparound porch, one dark eyebrow arching as she caught sight of Gabe pulling his bags from the bench seat of the truck. She rose and met them at the sidewalk.

"Moving in?" she asked.

Chapter Nine

"There's been a development," Gabe answered his niece's query, tersely filling her in on the mysterious messages from the killer.

Cissy's face blanched and she moved closer to Alicia, putting a protective hand on her shoulder. She shook her head, gazing at her uncle in consternation. "This is crazy! The killers haven't ever left messages before, have they?"

Alicia told her their theory about the beta killer being someone Alicia knew. Cissy's face went even paler.

"He could be a student?"

"We always knew that was possible," Alicia pointed out, starting up the steps to her apartment.

Cissy stayed in step. "Yeah, possible. But now it seems probable. Maybe not a student, but someone connected with the university." She shuddered as she waited for Alicia to unlock her apartment door. "That whole place is filled with women fitting the profile. It must look like a buffet to him."

Gabe stepped forward, putting his hand on Alicia's wrist as she started to open the door. He pulled his pistol from the holster at his waist. "Let me go in first."

Alicia exchanged a glance with Cissy, expecting the younger woman to be as amused by Gabe's macho posturing as she was. But Cissy's deadly serious expression had a sobering effect, and by the time Gabe gave them the all clear, Alicia's stomach had twisted into a dozen new knots.

"Where's a good place for takeout around here?" Gabe asked Cissy as he locked the door behind them.

"Brandywine Deli down the street is good. Great sandwiches priced with college students in mind. We can call in the order and I could go pick it up—"

"Do they deliver? I don't want you driving there alone."

Cissy frowned. "I don't fit the profile."

"You're close enough," he said firmly. "If something happened to you and I had to call your father—" The look on Gabe's face made Alicia's stomach hurt more than ever.

"They don't deliver, but if you can pony up a little extra cash for more sandwiches, I could probably talk a couple of my roommates into going with me."

Gabe fished in his pocket for his wallet and handed Cissy a pair of twenties. "Do they have a good Reuben?"

Cissy grinned, color seeping back into her face. "The best. Alicia, do you want your regular turkey on wheat?"

Alicia grimaced. "I'm really not hungry."

Gabe's warm hand closed over her shoulder. "You haven't eaten in hours."

"I know, but—"

"Food is fuel," Gabe said firmly. Cissy chuckled softly and he shot her a quick grin.

"Inside joke?" Alicia asked.

"Just something Granddad says all the time," Cissy explained with a smile.

"This is the Marine Corps sniper?" Alicia asked, remembering what Gabe had told her earlier.

"That's the one." Gabe dropped his hand away from her

shoulder. "If you're not up for a sandwich, at least get some soup or something."

"They have great chicken corn chowder," Cissy reminded her. "And the Tuscan tomato is yummy."

Being double-teamed by a pair of Coopers proved to be impossible to resist. Alicia had to wonder what it would be like to cross swords with the entire Cooper clan. No wonder they'd been able to fight off a deadly drug cartel. "Okay, I'll take a bowl of the chowder," she relented.

Both Coopers grinned back at her, lightening her own mood considerably. She was starting to feel hungry by the time Gabe let Cissy out and locked the door behind her.

"Look, I know this is a big imposition," Gabe started.

"You're protecting me. For free." She waved her hand toward the sofa, suggesting they sit. "I don't know how to thank you, really."

"We could start by letting me take a look at your files."

He was relentless; she had to give him that. "Fine. But wait until after dinner. Those files can ruin your appetite."

His smile faded. "I know."

Of course he would. He'd stumbled onto two of the crime scenes while they were still fresh. Smelled the blood, seen the carnage, felt the half-warmth of a body slowly assuming room temperature. No photograph could replicate that experience.

"You know what? Let's just think about something else for a little while." Gabe scanned the apartment. "Do you have a deck of cards?"

She furrowed her brow, trying to follow his swift change of subject. "Yeah, somewhere around here."

"Great!" He grinned up at her. "Find them and I'll teach you a fun new game."

She wasn't sure she trusted the wicked look in his eyes,

but she was up for anything that would take her mind off the threat hanging over her head. She headed in search of cards.

"It's called Popsmack and it's very easy to play." Gabe dealt the deck of cards evenly between them.

"Popsmack?"

He grinned. "Long story. It's something my brother Jake and I made up on a rainy afternoon when the folks wouldn't let us out on the water. Because of the lightning."

"Yeah, I could see where being on the water during a lightning storm might not be wise."

He shot her a quick look, grinning. "Chicken."

"Is Jake older or younger?"

"Older. By ten minutes. And he never lets me forget it."

"Oh, twins. Identical or fraternal?"

"Fraternal, although we look enough alike that people who don't know us well get us mixed up."

She couldn't imagine mistaking anyone for Gabe Cooper. "Do you have that twin vibe thing people talk about?"

"I'm not sure I believe in that stuff, but I do seem to know when something's not right with Jake. And vice versa." Gabe dealt the last card and sat back. "Okay, here's how the game works. We lay out one card at a time. The person with the high card gets to ask the person with the low card any question he wants. And the loser has to answer truthfully."

She saw danger written all over this game. But a different kind of danger than lurked outside her small apartment. A kind of danger that was so tempting, she could feel her blood singing at the prospect.

"Ready?" He asked.

She nodded, a nervous bubble rising in her throat.

He laid out a card. Jack of spades. Her heart gave a little dip, then began to race as she laid a six of clubs on the table between them. She looked up at him, waiting for his question with a mixture of dread and anticipation.

He met her gaze, silent for a long moment. His eyes glittered with wicked delight, as if he was contemplating just how naughty a question he could ask. By the time he finally spoke, her whole body was vibrating with tension.

"Why criminal psychology?"

She gave a small start of surprise, nearly overbalancing on her ottoman perch. She clutched the cushion to steady herself and wondered how to answer his unexpectedly serious question without baring parts of her soul she'd never shared with anyone.

She decided to go with part of the truth. "Rebellion."

"Against your parents? Or your brother?"

"I thought it was just one question per deal."

He smiled. "Fair enough." He laid down another card. Three of hearts.

She smiled back as she laid down a ten of clubs. "Have you ever been in love?"

"Right to the money question, huh? You women are so predictable."

"Trying to avoid the question?"

"No." He sighed, running his finger around the edge of the card he'd dealt. "I thought I was in love in high school. Mary Beth Traylor. Cutest majorette on the team. Really good with her hands."

Alicia groaned at the innuendo.

"No, seriously," Gabe said, although the gleam in his eyes was anything but sincere. "She was a runner-up in the Miss Alabama pageant about ten years ago. Twirled a mean baton."

"So why didn't you marry Miss Almost Alabama?"

"She met a plastic surgeon who was mad about her.

How could a country boy who spent his day catching fish compete with something like that?"

"You dumped her?"

"Entirely too high maintenance. I'd have gone broke from the hair spray bill alone."

Grinning, she laid down another card. "Oh, look. A queen."

He flipped over a card and grinned. "Oh, look. A king."

She eyed him suspiciously, not liking the way he was looking at her. "I'm not sure you don't have this deck stacked in your favor."

"Cheating at Popsmack is a hanging offense. I would never besmirch the honor of the game that way." He toyed with the card in front of him, a thoughtful look on his face. Finally, his gaze whipped up to meet hers, surprisingly serious. "Rebellion against whom?"

A sex question would have been less painful to answer, she thought, nudging her inadequate queen of diamonds toward the middle of the coffee table. "Both my parents and my brother, I guess. I was determined not to be like any of them."

She could see him itching to ask a follow-up question, but she thwarted him by setting her stack of cards on the table and getting up, walking over to look out the window. Night was falling fast, making her wonder if she and Gabe had made a mistake by sending Cissy off for food with dusk so close.

"I wonder what's taking Cissy so long?"

"It's been only ten minutes." Gabe's voice was so close she jumped. Turning, she found him standing right behind her, so close that her arm brushed against his hard-muscled abdomen when she turned.

He didn't move away and the expression on his face

suggested he had no intention of doing so. His eyes had turned a smoky blue that reminded her of the color of San Francisco Bay when a storm was brewing in the Pacific.

His head bent closer. "I'm going to kiss you now. If you want me to stop, say so now."

Her throat seemed to close, rebelling against the warning signals blaring from her brain.

She didn't want him to stop.

Gabe dipped his head lower, his lips brushing hers. The touch was light and undemanding. A taste, as if offering a sample to see if she wanted more. And she did.

Sliding her fingers into the crisp, dark hair at the back of his head, she drew him down to her, lips parting in invitation. Then his lips claimed hers and the world spun out of control.

His real name wasn't Karl Avalon, but he'd gone by that moniker over the last few years when he was in hunting mode. Alex had given him the name, after a dog he'd had as a boy—and tortured to death. Alex had found the idea amusing and Karl had gone along because there was usually no upside to crossing Alex.

He'd never made Victor change his name, as far as Karl knew. He didn't know what that meant.

He didn't know a lot about Alex, really. Karl had found his partner by way of Victor, who'd let a few clues slip during their discussions at the Southern Mississippi Correctional Institution, where Victor had been doing three to five on a vehicular manslaughter charge.

He'd found Alex in the middle of a murder and helped him clean up the mess, winning his chance at taking Victor's place. It had been a satisfying partnership, for the most part.

He was finding his role as point man a bit tedious.

Across the street, now that dusk had fallen, the lights inside Alicia Solano's apartment gave off warm, golden light. She and the man he now knew was Gabe Cooper had entered a little while earlier, along with Alicia's student, Cissy. Cissy had left with a couple of her roommates a few minutes later. Alicia was alone with Cooper.

It hadn't taken long for word about the visitor to spread in the small, insular town of Millbridge. It turned out that Cooper was a minor celebrity among fishing enthusiasts, having won a couple of big money bass tournaments a few years back. Of course, Karl knew about Gabe Cooper by name already.

His brother Jake had come close to ruining everything only a month earlier, thanks to Victor Logan's foolish incompetence.

But Karl had taken care of things. Victor was dead. Any evidence that might have linked Victor to Alex had perished when Victor's house burned to the ground.

Unlike Victor, Karl knew how to get things done.

Victor's emotions had gotten in his way. His obsession with Mariah Cooper had cost him everything. Karl knew better than to let his own emotions get in the way.

His interest in Alicia Solano wasn't emotional. It certainly wasn't love, that desperate construct of a human mind so weak it had to seek ephemeral connections to keep from imploding into madness.

Powerful people didn't need connections. They needed only the resources that thrived within themselves. He'd learned that lesson long before he met Alex and recognized a fellow traveler.

He didn't depend on Alex for anything. Their partnership was a mutual arrangement that suited their individual needs, or it had done so thus far. As he'd noted before, he was getting tired of being left out of the kills.

That's why he'd chosen Alicia as his own personal side project.

Movement in her apartment window drew his gaze. He saw her silhouette darken the square of light. The curtains were closed, but he saw one move aside, and though she was backlit too much for him to make out her features, he imagined her there, filling in the blanks from memory.

Suddenly a second silhouette loomed behind her. He saw her turn and then the two shapes blended into one.

A strange sensation crawled through his chest as he realized what was happening.

He looked away, sickened.

ALICIA'S MOUTH WAS SOFT. Fiery hot and sweet as sin. He had joked before about Mary Beth Traylor's talented hands, but the majorette had nothing on Alicia, whose nimble fingers were doing all sorts of crazy good things to the muscles of his back. Wrapping his arms around her waist, he dragged her closer, until her firm breasts pressed hard against his chest and her hips cradled the growing hardness beneath the zipper of his jeans.

She dragged her mouth away from his, her breath escaping in short, sharp gasps. "Cissy's coming back, you know."

He nipped at the curve of her earlobe with his teeth. "I know. But she doesn't have a key."

"So we just keep making out while your niece bangs on the door?" She clutched his shoulders suddenly, sagging a little as his lips left her ear behind and moved down the side of her neck. He tightened his grip on her, keeping her upright.

For the moment, anyway.

She pushed against his shoulders. "Gabe, we can't do this. You know we can't."

He knew no such thing, but he wasn't the kind of guy to push himself on a woman who was saying *no,* even when her lush, hot body was screaming *yes* against his. Gathering his self-control, he let her go and she stumbled back, catching herself against the wall by the window.

She was still breathing hard, her hair tousled by his hands and her cheeks and neck bright pink from his kisses. Her coal-dark eyes met his, liquid and full of need. It took every bit of strength Gabe had not to close the distance between them and pick up where he left off.

"We need to set some ground rules—" she began. But a knock on the door interrupted.

With a low groan of frustration, Gabe crossed to the door and checked the security lens. It was Cissy, holding two large white bags.

"Cissy," he muttered, glancing at Alicia. She straightened her clothes and pushed her hair back from her face, shooting a desperate look his direction.

"Go sit on the sofa," he murmured. She did as he suggested. He waited until she'd settled down and composed herself—and his own body was back in check—before he released the lock and let his niece inside.

"We didn't discuss dessert," Cissy said, carrying the bags to the kitchen counter, "but they had a fresh Mississippi mud cake, and I couldn't resist getting a couple of pieces."

Alicia crossed to the sink and washed her hands, taking the opportunity to pat her pink cheeks with cool water. "You're an enabler for my chocolate addiction, Cissy. Maybe you should sit in on the class I teach about codependency."

Gabe felt his body cooling enough that he could safely cross to the counter, close enough to touch Alicia, and remain under control. But it took a little effort to keep his mind off the way her ripe, curvy body had felt against his, soft and hard in all the right places.

Cissy had been right; the food from Brandywine Deli was as delicious as advertised. His Reuben was as good as any he'd ever tasted. Alicia poured them all glasses of cold, sweet tea and they capped the meal with the Mississippi mud cake, the rich, decadent combination of earthy chocolate icing and gooey marshmallow enough to satisfy any sweet tooth.

As she licked the last bit of chocolate from her spoon, Cissy's gaze wandered to the coffee table in front of the sofa. She shot Gabe a grin. "You were playing Popsmack?"

"Gabe thought it would get our mind off things," Alicia murmured, her dark-eyed gaze sliding up to meet Gabe's.

"Oh, Alicia, you might as well have stuck your head in a lion's mouth," Cissy admonished with a grin. "Uncle Gabe and Uncle Jake invented the game to torment each other. They use it for evil, believe me."

Alicia looked at him again, her eyes smoldering.

"I was good," Gabe lied, dragging his attention back to his niece. In between getting hot and bothered by Alicia, he'd also had a few moments to think about the possible dangers to his niece from the serial killer. She didn't fit the profile, exactly; she was curvy and dark-haired, yes, but also green-eyed, not brown-eyed, and only nineteen, a good six or seven years younger than the other victims.

Still, if their theory about the beta killer was right, he was already going off script in sending messages to Alicia. He was unpredictable, which made him doubly dangerous.

"Cissy, when's your final exam this semester?" he asked.

His niece gave him an odd look. "Tomorrow."

"Good. I want you to be packed and ready to go back to Gossamer Ridge by the time it's over."

Cissy frowned at him. "I can't. You know that. I'm working that internship at the police department this summer. It's all planned."

"It can be unplanned," he said firmly. "This town is too dangerous right now."

"I don't fit the profile."

"Maybe not for the alpha killer, but we think the beta is the one behind the messages to Alicia. Think about it—the victim profile is part of the alpha killer's signature, right?"

Cissy's expression darkened. "Yeah, but—"

"No buts. The beta may have a completely different motivation for his actions."

"Gabe's right," Alicia agreed. "The beta's made things personal by contacting me. That suggests a different signature. He's not following the alpha's playbook."

"He might hurt you to punish Alicia," Gabe added.

"I don't want to run away just because things are a little dangerous," Cissy insisted. "You know I want to work in law enforcement. What kind of cop would I be if I cut and run at the first sign of danger?"

"A live one," Gabe said.

"No." Cissy shook her head. "I'm careful. I'll make sure I don't go anywhere alone. I have a license to carry a concealed weapon, so I'll start doing that, at least when I'm off campus."

"Cissy—"

"I'm not a child. Not anymore."

Gabe stared at his niece, frustration burning in the center of his chest. He understood her need to stand her ground, admired her for it, even, but just the thought of something happening to her was enough to make his blood run cold.

"Why don't we table this discussion until after her last

exam tomorrow?" Alicia suggested quickly. "I think we've all had enough stress today."

Gabe squelched the urge to argue further, rising from the table to expend the tension roiling inside him like a building storm. He gathered up the detritus of their take-out meal and deposited it in the trash can in the kitchen, pausing at the window over the sink when movement outside caught his eye.

He stepped closer, pushing the curtain back further. There it was again. Movement in the shadows across the street. He made out a dark human form weaving in and out of the graceful draping branches of the willow trees lining the undeveloped no-man's-land on the other side of the street.

Suddenly, the silhouette disappeared.

Gabe muttered a profanity, wheeling and heading for the front door.

"What is it?" Alicia caught up with him at the door.

"Go with Cissy to her place—your roommates are all there, right?" He unlocked the door and threw it open.

"At least two of them," Cissy confirmed.

"What did you see?" Alicia asked.

"Someone hiding across the street in the trees," he said.

Chapter Ten

"I should go with you," Alicia insisted as Gabe ran down the steps.

"No." Gabe turned at the bottom of the steps. "I don't have time to argue. Go with Cissy."

He could see she was spoiling for a fight, and he might enjoy going toe-to-toe with her under any other circumstances. But for now, he just turned and raced across the street, seeking the last place he'd seen the dark figure before it disappeared.

It didn't take long to figure out where he'd gone. There was a river-stone and concrete retaining wall at the top of a shallow incline, separating the stand of willows from a narrow alley that ran behind the gas station on the corner of Dogwood and University. Gazing down the shadowy alley, Gabe spotted a figure turn the corner and disappear behind a house near the end of the alley.

He was too far away to catch, but that didn't keep Gabe from racing toward the next cross street to see if he could spot the dark figure emerging from between the houses. But by the time he reached the next street, there was nothing to see. No movement, not even people out in their yards or arriving home late from work.

Muttering a low, frustrated profanity, he headed back for the alley and followed it down to the house where he'd seen the dark figure disappear around the corner. It was an older house, probably built around the same time as Belleview Manor, a comfortably shabby two-story home with a large screened-in back porch. There were lights on inside the house and the sound of loud music with a heavy bass beat.

Gabe circled the house and knocked on the front door. A few seconds later, it opened and a bleary-eyed guy in his late teens stared at him.

Drunk or stoned, Gabe diagnosed as the kid swayed toward him, catching the door frame to keep from falling. "Yeah? What do you want?"

Gabe was tempted to identify himself as a cop, just to see the kid's reaction. Instead, he got to the point. "Did you see anyone cross your side yard a few minutes ago?"

The kid just started laughing and closed the door in Gabe's face. Gabe released a frustrated chuckle himself and started trudging back toward Alicia's apartment.

He spotted Alicia and Cissy, along with three other girls, sitting on the front porch. They'd turned on all the porch lights, lighting up the apartment building like an airport runway.

Cissy and Alicia broke away from the others and met him halfway up the sidewalk. "Did you find anything?" Alicia asked.

"There was someone running down the alley. I'm pretty sure it was a male. He had a big head start and I couldn't catch up." Gabe walked with them back to where his truck was parked by the curb. He gestured toward the willows. "I think he might have been watching the apartment from under those trees."

"Watching us?" Alicia asked as he unlocked the truck.

He glanced at her, knowing what she was asking. They'd been standing in the window when they kissed. The curtains had been closed, but he could tell at a glance that their silhouettes would have been readily visible to anyone watching from across the street.

"Probably." He opened the truck's glove compartment and retrieved a large flashlight. "Y'all go back inside. I'll be just a minute."

"Go inside with the others," Alicia told Cissy. "I'll help Gabe look around."

He started to protest, but the set of her chin told him arguing would be pointless. He gestured with his head for Cissy to do as Alicia asked. Fire flickered in her green eyes but she gathered up the other girls and went back into her apartment without putting up an argument.

"So, do you suppose it was the beta or the alpha?" Alicia asked when they reached the other side of the street.

"Might have been your run-of-the-mill Peeping Tom."

"You don't believe that."

Not answering, he ran the beam of the flashlight across the ground beneath the willows. Fallen leaves from previous autumns still littered the area beneath the trees like a loamy carpet. He couldn't see any signs of footprints or anything else that might help them identify the mystery man he'd spotted.

"If it's the beta, he's not going to drop a convenient gum wrapper or a cigarette butt with his DNA still attached," Alicia murmured. "They've gotten away with murder for a long time."

"The alpha has. We're pretty sure he switched betas when Victor went to jail," he reminded her.

"Still, that's over four years of committing murders and not leaving any evidence behind. I don't think the alpha would pair up with someone he didn't know could be trusted to cover his own tracks."

They scanned the area for a few more minutes, without

luck. Gabe finally switched off the flashlight, plunging the ground beneath the willows into shadows again.

He felt Alicia move closer to him, instinctively seeking him out in the sudden darkness. He wondered if she even realized what she was doing.

She was afraid. She'd be a fool not to be.

He was afraid for her.

"Let's go back to the apartment." He caught her hand, surprised to find her fingers icy cold. He closed his fingers over hers, warming them as they walked back to the apartment.

He locked them safely inside and turned to look at her, releasing her hand. "You understand that Cissy has to leave tomorrow, don't you?"

She crossed her arms, tucking her hands beneath her elbows as if to warm them. "You're right. The beta's unpredictable, and if he knows the subject of my doctoral dissertation, then he probably knows that Cissy and I are friends."

Gabe led the way to the sofa and sat, gazing up at her. "He may even know who I am. This is a small town, and between my run-ins with the cops and my connection to Cissy, word could have spread fast."

"I think we have to assume he does know who you are." She sat close to him. Too close. He felt his temperature notch upward as her arm brushed his. "It won't take long for him to connect you to Brenda Cooper's murder, either."

"Or what happened last month in Mississippi," he added.

"I read up on that and Cissy filled in some blanks for me. It sounds like a pretty horrible ordeal." She leaned a little closer, her side now nestled against his. He felt awkward sitting there elbow to elbow so he lifted his arm and draped it over the back of the sofa behind her.

"My brother and his wife had a rough time of it," Gabe agreed. Jake and Mariah had been taken captive at gunpoint by Victor Logan and barely escaped with their lives after a harrowing cat and mouse chase through the rainy Mississippi woods for a couple of days.

She glanced at him, a flicker of humor in her dark eyes. "I know at the time it happened, nobody was thinking in terms of an alpha killer and a beta killer, but do you think it's possible that the second man your brother and sister-in-law saw—the one you said had a rifle—could be the beta we're looking for in these murders?"

Gabe hadn't really considered that possibility before now. No one had been able to figure out the identity of the mystery gunman Jake and Mariah had encountered during their escape from Victor. Neither of them had gotten a good look at his face, so all they'd been able to tell the authorities and the rest of the Cooper family was that the man with the rifle—the man who'd rigged the gas explosion that had killed Victor and destroyed his house—had sandy brown hair and a lean build and youthful way of moving.

Except for the sandy hair—because the darkness outside had obscured any details like coloring—that description of the gunman sounded a hell of a lot like the dark figure he'd seen lurking outside Alicia's apartment earlier.

"Okay, let's say it's the same guy. The rifleman in Buckley, Mississippi, is the same guy who sent you a note and was just now lurking outside your apartment," Gabe agreed. "What does that tell us about him?"

"Well, if we're assuming that he lives in the area where he hunts for victims for the alpha killer, I'd say that means he lived in the Buckley area at least for a while last month."

"Not necessarily," Gabe said, remembering something about the events that had unfolded for his family the previous month. "This all took place the first week of April. And what I remember about that week, besides what happened to Jake and Mariah, is that Cissy was home from college on a break."

Alicia's eyes widened. "That's right. We do take a later spring break than a lot of colleges. So the beta could still have been living here at the time. He could have been in the Buckley area for the break." Her brow creased. "But why? How did he know to be in Buckley at just that time?"

A light went on in Gabe's brain. "Of course. The cable news broadcast."

Alicia's frown deepened. "What broadcast?"

"One of the cable news outlets carried a live broadcast from the tornado sites. When we did a little looking into how Victor Logan could have known Mariah was in Buckley, the cops talked the local stations and the cable newsers into letting us look at the footage they aired the day after the twister hit. We found a couple of hits—one with just Mariah and Jake in the background of an on-scene live report, and a later one from a cable news station that showed Victor actually stalking Mariah and Jake."

"So if the beta knew Victor—"

"Oh, he knew him," Gabe said confidently. "My guess is that he knew Victor first and maybe that's how he ended up hooking up with the alpha."

"Possibly," Alicia agreed. "So if he knew Victor, and he saw Victor stalking people on a national cable broadcast—"

"He'd probably want to know what the hell Victor was up to," Gabe finished for her. "Jake and Mariah said the guy seemed to be Victor's ally sometimes and his enemy at other times. Very strange relationship."

"Very strange seems to be our beta's primary descriptor," Alicia said dryly.

"And very dangerous," Gabe added. "Because if we're

right, then he's one hell of a determined freak. And right now, he seems pretty damned determined to see you dead."

TONY EVANS WAS OFF DUTY when Alicia reached him on his cell phone, but he came to her apartment as quickly as he could. He eyed Gabe with a little bit of latent hostility as soon as he stepped out of his car, but Alicia forced Tony's attention to the issue of the stalker.

"You're right," he said a few minutes later after examining the area under the willows that she and Gabe had already investigated. "The area's pretty clean. I'm not sure even a crime scene team could get anything here. I doubt I could get permission to call a team out here tonight in any event. Some guy standing across the street from an apartment full of pretty girls may be creepy, but it's not illegal."

Gabe shot Alicia an *I-told-you-so* look. He had been against calling Tony, certain the police couldn't do anything about a guy who hadn't broken any laws.

"I do think it's interesting he was on foot," Tony added. "Sounds like he could live around here."

"Or he's smart enough to park his car a couple of blocks away so that nobody can connect him to some strange vehicle parked outside Alicia's place," Gabe added.

Tony shot him a dark look. "Or that," he conceded.

Alicia looked at Gabe, whose glittering eyes were locked in battle with Tony's. "Did the guy see you chasing him?"

Gabe turned his attention to her. "No, I'm pretty sure he didn't see me. By the time I was able to get outside and go after him, I was too far behind for him to notice."

"So maybe he'll come back. At least we know where to look for him."

"I don't think you should try to take on the guy yourself,"

Tony warned. "I mean, I know Gabe here is an auxiliary deputy and all, but this guy could be really dangerous."

Alicia nearly rolled her eyes at Tony's barely veiled insult of Gabe's part-time law enforcement work. "Believe me, we know how dangerous he could be."

"Sorry to drag you out here, Tony," Gabe said, clapping Tony on the shoulder. "I guess we were being overly cautious and all. Not being professionals like you."

Alicia groaned inwardly. *Oh, for God's sake, what was it with men?*

"Well, anything for my girl Alicia here." Tony wrapped his arm around her and hugged her to him. Under most circumstances, the gesture would have been innocent enough, but choking on the cloud of testosterone emanating from the two men, Alicia saw it for the territorial gesture it was.

She extricated herself firmly from his grasp. "I'll try not to call you out on a wild goose chase next time, Tony. Thanks for coming."

Tony's eyes narrowed, but he got the message and said his goodbyes at the curb, though he did eye the front door of her apartment as if he would have liked to be invited in.

Alicia felt a little guilty for excluding him, but their relationship was over and she wasn't interested in stirring up old embers. She had enough trouble on her plate as it was.

Gabe laid his hand on the small of her back, guiding her toward the steps. It was just as territorial a gesture as Tony's quick hug, but Alicia didn't find it nearly as irritating. After all, Gabe was here to protect her. He did have a stake in what happened to her.

And if going all alpha male was his way of keeping focused on that job, Alicia wasn't inclined to complain.

They had barely stepped inside the apartment when the phone began to ring. Tony, calling to make sure she was safely inside, maybe? Alicia picked up the receiver and checked the caller ID on the wireless phone's display. Nothing showed up; the caller must have blocked his information from displaying.

She was about to push the answer button when Gabe caught her wrist, making her arm tingle from fingertips to shoulder.

She looked up at him, every inch of her body aware of just how close he was standing. "What?"

"It could be the beta, sending another message," he murmured. "Do you have another extension?"

Her heart skipped a beat. She should have thought of that possibility herself. "In the bedroom."

"Wait 'til you hear me say go." He disappeared down the hall. A second later, he called out, "Go."

She answered the phone. "Hello?"

"Oh, thank God. I was afraid I'd have to leave a message on your answering machine and you know how much I hate those bloody things."

Alicia's heart sank. "Hi, Mom."

There was a soft click on the line. Gabe hanging up the phone, now that he knew it wasn't a call from a killer.

"What was that?" Lorraine Betts-Solano asked. "Was that someone else on the line?"

Alicia pressed her fingertips to her forehead and ignored the question. "How's Dad? Is he there?"

"He's still at work—late seminar. Don't change the subject. Do you have a roommate now?"

"No, Mom, no roommate."

"You're not back with that police officer again, are you?" Lorraine didn't bother to hide her disdain.

"No, it's not Tony."

"But it's someone."

Alicia shook her head. For all the pride she took in being an unconventional, untraditional woman, her mother was every bit as obsessed with Alicia's love life as a mother whose primary goal was seeing her daughter well-married.

Of course, Lorraine's interest was in making sure Alicia didn't settle for someone unsuitable for Martin and Lorraine Solano's daughter. Police officers were a definite no. Nor had they approved of the stockbroker she'd dated for a while when she was attending grad school in New York.

Feeling a wicked streak of rebellion, she blurted, "If you have to know, he's a professional fisherman. I met him through one of my students—he's her uncle."

There was dead silence on the other end of the line.

"He's from right here in Alabama," she added, pouring it on. She knew her mother's opinion of any place that didn't have its own public transit system and a visible skyline.

"When you say professional fisherman—"

"He fishes for a living. Owns a bass boat, takes people out and shows them where to catch fish. I think he said he's fished a few tournaments, too."

"Dear God, where do you meet these people? Never mind, I know where you meet them. Why you ever chose a little no-name college for your doctorate—"

"It's a university, not a college," Alicia said firmly. "Mill Valley is quite prestigious in the region. I went where my subject matter was."

"Oh, yes, your beloved murderers."

"At least I don't date them."

"Small comfort, Alicia. Your father and I still believe you're wasting the talents and opportunities you're fortunate enough to have at your disposal."

"You mean I'm not doing what you and Dad think I should be doing," Alicia corrected.

"Your obsession with the picayune and the grotesque was amusing when you were a teenager. But you're not a teenager anymore. It's time to take your rightful place—"

"You make our family sound like royalty, Mother." Alicia chose the word deliberately, knowing which buttons to push. "Have you and Dad found a suitable match for me from a neighboring realm?"

"I have nothing against your fisherman, nor your policeman for that matter. Their work is noble enough, but surely you can see that your opportunities for conversation, for mutual stimulation is severely limited—"

"I can assure you, there's no limit to our mutual stimulation," Alicia retorted, blushing even as she said it. Her mother had urged her to speak honestly and openly about her sexuality. But Alicia knew that Lorraine didn't really want to hear the details of her daughter's love life any more than Alicia wanted to share them.

"Your attempts to embarrass me won't work," Lorraine said. But Alicia could hear the unease in her voice. "Does your fishmonger have any sort of college education? What about his parents? What sort of living wage can he possibly make at such an occupation? You can't live off your fellowship forever."

"I don't know if he has a college education. I've never met his parents. And I suppose his income would depend on just how good a fisherman he is." She shifted positions, turning toward the bedroom, and found herself face-to-face with Gabe, who stood in the doorway to the hall, his large frame filling the opening. The look in his eyes left her with no doubt that he'd been there long enough to overhear her conversation with her mother and accurately guess what her mother had said in return.

"Four years of college, great parents, enough money to own a house outright," he murmured softly. "Any more questions?"

"Mom, I need to go. I'll call you later." She waited just

long enough for her mother's goodbye and hung up the phone.

"Gabe, I'm so sorry—"

He shook his head. "No need. I'm not ashamed of what I do for a living. I'm good at it and I make good money." He pushed away from the doorway and crossed slowly toward her. "But I'll admit I'm a little interested in why you chose me and my fishing business to bait your mother."

Chapter Eleven

Alicia stared at Gabe for a second, her cheeks flushing prettily pink. Though he still felt a little annoyed that she'd used him as a tool of rebellion, he wasn't immune to her ample charms, including the girlish chagrin that tinted her voice when she answered, "Because I'm apparently a teenager still getting her rocks off by making her mother lose her cool?"

"I'll go out on a limb here and guess your mom doesn't approve of what you're doing with your life."

"Oh, she wanted me to be in academia like she and Dad are, but no, my field of study isn't anywhere near her list of acceptable areas of expertise." Alicia dropped wearily to the sofa. She looked as tired as Gabe felt, and it was no wonder, after her stressful day. Clearly her mother's call hadn't done anything to soothe her shattered nerves.

"She thought you'd follow her and your father into political activism?"

Laying her head back on the sofa, she looked up at him. "Except I've made it a rule to avoid politics like the plague, at least as a topic of conversation or a choice of majors."

"That must have made your home life pleasant."

"A Solano who'd rather read books on criminal profiling than march on downtown San Francisco in the protest du jour? Yeah, I was real popular."

"I guess that'd be like a Cooper who didn't like to fish." He sat next to her, close but not touching.

She slanted a wry look his way. "*Are* there any Coopers who don't like to fish?"

"Hell, no!" he answered with indignation.

She chuckled.

"But fishing isn't the same as being notorious for anti-government activities or being an international terrorist," he added more soberly.

"No. It's not." He could see reluctance in her expression, as if she wanted to end the conversation here. He knew a lot about her family life, at least the part that had played out in newspaper articles during her brother's time on the FBI's Most Wanted list. He wondered how much worse the story got.

He saw the moment she made up her mind to tell him more. Her expression cleared and her dark eyes widened with vulnerability but also with hope, as if she was counting on him to understand what she was about to tell him.

He hoped he'd do justice to her faith.

"I've spent my whole life dealing with fans and foes of my family," she said. "There doesn't seem to be much middle ground where they're concerned."

"Except you. You're the middle ground."

"Exactly." She looked up at him, her eyes shining with gratitude. He wondered what she was grateful for. His understanding her situation? Had she received so little sympathy in her life that she found his common kindness noteworthy?

He felt a rush of pure pity for her, but quickly hid the emotion when he saw uncertainty fill her dark eyes.

He cleared his throat. "I'm guessing the fans would be people you've met on your job, right? Professors and students who idolize your parents for their brilliant scholarship and their ideas?"

She nodded. "They're always so surprised when I don't want to discuss my parents or their work. Or sometimes they judge me by my parents and find my own ideas and beliefs sadly lacking in countercultural verve." Alicia kicked off her shoes and propped her feet on the coffee table in front of her. "I've had some teachers offer to give me extra credit if I could just introduce them to my parents."

Gabe grimaced. "Jerks."

She lifted her chin. "Not that I needed their damned extra credit. I've never coasted on my parents' reputation."

"No, I can't imagine you doing that," Gabe agreed. "I suppose the foes you were talking about are the law enforcement types you deal with in your field of study?"

She sighed. "I don't think there's a police department in this country small enough to be unfamiliar with the name Sinclair Solano. Or Martin and Lorraine Solano, for that matter. I mean, my parents literally wrote the book on defying the police to achieve their idea of social justice. They're not exactly popular with cops."

"And you get painted with that brush, too?"

She nodded. "The stupid thing is, I never approved of what Sinclair was doing in Sanselmo. Ever. Even when my parents were ambivalent, I wasn't. I'd done my homework— I knew *El Cambio* was worse than the government they were trying to overthrow, no matter what their flowery rhetoric might suggest." As if realizing Gabe might not have a clue what she was talking about, she added, "*El Cambio* was the rebel group in Sanselmo that my brother was working with to overthrow the Cardenas government—"

"I know," Gabe said quickly. "Remember when Tony and I were talking about that mess my family had to deal with last year? One of the groups we had to fight off had connections to *El Cambio*. Two of my brothers were in the Marines—they both had nasty dealings with *El Cambio* and the connected drug cartels in Sanselmo. And for what it's worth, I agree with you—as bad as Cardenas was, *El Cambio* is worse."

"I guess one good thing came out of what happened to my brother," she murmured, pain sharp in her eyes. "The bomb that killed Sinclair ruined *El Cambio* in the eyes of the public that had been supporting them."

"It didn't hurt that Cardenas died of a heart attack just in time for a more moderate reformer to swoop in and pick up the slack." Gabe couldn't keep the cynicism out of his voice, but he softened his tone as he added, "It must have been hard for you, losing your brother that way, half a world away, without even getting to say goodbye."

Tears filled her eyes. "But I did say goodbye."

"You were in contact with him at that point?" Gabe asked when she didn't continue. He was surprised.

She stared at him, conflicting emotions playing across her expression. She released a shaky breath. "It was the night before he died. I hadn't heard from him in years and he called, out of the blue." She leaned forward, looking ill. "I was so surprised to hear from him, it took a minute to realize what he was trying to tell me."

"What was he trying to tell you?" Gabe asked, moving his hand in comforting circles over her back.

"He wanted me to understand why he was doing what he was doing in Sanselmo. I don't know, maybe he was asking me to forgive and forget." She buried her face in her palms. "I didn't let him get that far. I told him not to call me again. As far as I was concerned, he was dead. Then I said I hoped he blew himself up the next time he set one of his stupid bombs."

Gabe groaned in sympathy.

"That was the last thing I said to my brother." Tears spilled down her cheeks. She dashed them away, as if angry at her weakness. "What if I was the reason—?"

"You weren't," Gabe said firmly. "Anything that happened to your brother happened because of his own choices and actions. You know that."

"It haunts me. Every day. Any time I think of Sin."

Regret burned in his gut like acid. "There are always going to be things we do or say that we can't take back. So we just live with the consequences the best we can."

"How do you live with it?" she asked aloud.

He knew she didn't know the full story of his involvement in Brenda's death, but her question was so pointed, it hit the sore spot festering in his gut, making him flinch.

He found his voice after a couple of seconds. "You just get up in the morning, do what you have to do and try to get enough sleep that night to do it all over again the next day."

She frowned at his answer, as if she didn't like what he had to say. "Where's the joy and the meaning? I can't live that way. No one can."

Gabe rose to his feet and moved restlessly to the window, gazing out into the darkness as he searched for a reason to leave this heavy conversation behind.

"Do you see anything out there?" Alicia asked.

He shook his head. "I think he's gone for tonight."

"Maybe he'll come back tomorrow night and we'll catch him."

"Maybe." Gabe didn't sound convinced. She wondered why.

He answered her unasked question a moment later, turning to look at her with a serious expression. "I know you're not going to want to hear this, but have you ever considered that it could be Tony who's stalking you?"

Alicia rose from the sofa, her dark eyes flashing with anger. She dodged the coffee table and crossed the floor to him in a few quick, purposeful steps. "Have you lost your mind?"

He stood his ground, remembering the stolen looks Tony had shot her way every time she wasn't looking. She might be over their former relationship, but Tony Evans clearly wasn't. "If we're going to be unbiased investigators, then we have to look at all the possibilities, not just the first one that fits."

"And you really think it's possible that Tony Evans was standing outside my apartment watching me tonight?"

"Yes. You couldn't reach him at home, right? You only got him on his cell phone."

"So, he was out having dinner or catching a movie or something. So what?"

"So, it took him maybe six minutes to get here. He was in the area when you called."

"Millbridge is about the size of a postage stamp. Everywhere in town is in the area," Alicia retorted, bristling like a sexy little porcupine.

Clearly, she was deeply loyal to anyone she chose to call a friend, a trait Gabe usually admired. But if her loyalty was getting in the way of seeing the situation clearly, she could end up getting badly burned.

"I'm not accusing Tony of anything here," Gabe clarified, trying a different approach. "All I'm saying is, it's worth considering the same potential suspects you'd want to take a look at if you were a cop working a stalker case. Tony is your ex-boyfriend. He's still in touch with you, still has feelings for you—"

"Not those kinds of feelings," Alicia insisted.

Gabe knew better, but he didn't argue. "Even so, if I were a cop, I'd still take a good, hard look at him."

"Why? Are you saying he's the beta killer? Because I can tell you right now, I can give him an alibi for the first two murders here in Millbridge."

"Not the beta, no," Gabe answered, trying not to wonder what, exactly, she and Tony had been doing together during the first two Millbridge murders. "But our mystery stalker hanging out across the street, watching your place? It's exactly the sort of behavior a jilted ex might indulge in."

"He wasn't jilted. The breakup was mutual."

"Who brought it up first?"

He saw the answer, heard it in her slight hesitation, before she answered. "I did. But he agreed."

Gabe couldn't imagine any man finding it easy to walk away from Alicia. Hell, he'd known her for one day and he already found himself thinking about her when she wasn't around. How much worse must it be for Tony Evans?

He'd met Gabe this afternoon at the crime scene. Maybe caught some of the sparks flying between him and Alicia. Could it have been enough to send him into stalker mode? Had he wanted to see for himself how Alicia and Gabe behaved when they were all alone at her place?

If so, they'd certainly given him an eyeful with that kiss at the window.

"Does your suspicion of Tony have anything to do with the fact that he's *my* ex?" Alicia asked.

Gabe wished he could say no, but he'd never been a good liar and she certainly didn't deserve deception. "If you're asking whether or not I'm being a territorial jerk, then the answer is…maybe."

Her lips curved slightly. "Fair enough."

"But setting that aside, I do think you have to be careful, even with people you know well."

She cocked her head, the half smile widening until it

carved delicious little dimples in her cheeks. "Or people I met a day ago?"

"Another fair point," he conceded. "And maybe it's a good idea for you to find out more about me before you entrust me with your safety. I'd probably start with the Chickasaw County Sheriff's Department. I had to go through some security clearance measures to join as an auxiliary and most of the people there know me and can vouch for me—"

She touched his arm. "I don't need to check up on you. I trust Cissy and she trusts you. That's enough."

"I don't know, Alicia." He frowned, wishing he could take pleasure in her obvious ease around him. "I want you to feel safe on one hand, but if you feel too safe, you'll start taking foolish risks—"

"I'll be careful. I'll go to work and I'll come home. Period. I won't give anyone a chance to get me alone." She dropped her hand from his arm. The air that filled the void felt cold and empty.

"Speaking of that, what's your schedule like tomorrow?"

"I have a couple of classes in the morning, a lab before lunch, then two labs right after lunch. Home by five, I promise." She flashed him a cheeky grin that made his whole body go blistering hot.

He knew he should back away, put distance between himself and the tempting little minx, but his mind seemed to have no control over the rest of him. He walked toward her slowly, watching with feral satisfaction as her pupils darkened and her lips parted as if anticipating his kiss.

Well, sweetheart, if you insist...

She put her hand up as if to push back against his chest, but almost as soon as her palm flattened against the front of his shirt, her fingers curled in the fabric and clung, pulling him closer. She rose on the tips of her toes and tilted her head back, her breath soft, chocolate-scented and warm against his cheek. "I'm going to kiss you now," she murmured, her voice velvety and low. He noticed that, while she mimicked the warning he gave her before their first kiss, she didn't offer him a chance to back out.

Fine with him.

Her mouth was hot and demanding, skipping any sort of introductory foray and moving straight to seduction. Gabe found himself losing all sense of equilibrium, something that he'd never experienced before. It was as if the world had stopped spinning, hurtling him into a void where there was no up or down, no in or out.

Alicia slid her hand beneath the hem of his shirt, her fingers cool against the hot skin of his back. She left a sizzling trail of electric sparks along the nerve endings where she traced the muscles of his back, almost distracting him completely from the maddening things her mouth and tongue were doing to his.

Suddenly, she made a groaning noise deep in her throat and lifted both hands to his chest, palms flat and firm. This time, she didn't clutch his shirt and pull him closer. She pushed away, dragging her lips from his, and took a couple of unsteady steps backwards.

"No," she breathed, scraping her hair out of her flushed face. She was still breathing hard, her rising and falling chest threatening to distract him from what she was saying. "No, no, no, I'm not going to do this."

"I think you already did," he murmured.

She shot him a blazing look. "It's the damned accent! And the way you Southern guys look at women like you can't decide if you want to take us to bed or put us on a pedestal. Which is so damned sexist, you know, and you really shouldn't do it, and I really shouldn't like it."

"But you do?"

A mewling sound of frustration escaped her lips. "Yes."

"And it's all because of my accent and the way I look at you? Nothing to do with me in particular. You jump any guy that drops an *R* or looks at you a certain way?"

"Yes. No!" She pressed her face into her hands, shoved her hair back again and raised her chin. He saw the moment she regained control of herself, when her hands stopped trembling and the steel in her spine asserted itself. She leveled her gaze with his, the heat gone, replaced by fierce determination.

It was about the sexiest thing he'd ever seen.

"There's a lot at stake here, Gabe. Not just for me but for you, for your brother, for Cissy and her little brother."

Her mention of his family had a quick, sobering effect on Gabe. He pushed aside the clamoring demands of his body and tried to mimic her self-control. "I know."

"If we keep doing this, we're going to lose focus. If we're not paying attention at some crucial juncture because our hormones are calling the shots—"

"I know," he repeated. "You're right."

"So we don't do this again. Agreed?"

"Never?" He felt his control starting to slip at the realization that he'd be spending the next few nights alone in the apartment with her. Her sofa had made a surprisingly comfortable bed, but he didn't think there was a bed on earth, no matter how lush and comfortable, that would help him sleep well tonight.

Not with Alicia sleeping one room away.

"I'm not a good relationship bet, Gabe. I'm obsessed with my work, I have family issues out the wazoo—and I don't do casual sex, so I'm not a good bet for a fling, either."

He didn't either, not these days. In fact, his out of control reaction to Alicia wasn't anything he'd ever experienced before and he wish he knew what the hell was causing it.

She was pretty enough, but he'd seen more beautiful women. Her curvy shape whispered all sorts of wicked promises about what lay beneath her clothing, but he'd seen perfect bodies before, clothed and unclothed, that hadn't tempted him this way.

What was wrong with him?

"Can we just agree to not do this? Please?" Alicia's voice softened. "I need your help. I need someone watching my back while I'm investigating this case. But we can't—"

"Okay," he said. "I will do my damnedest to be on my best behavior with you." *Even if it kills me,* he added silently.

"Thank you." She crossed warily to the sofa and sat down, her dark eyes watchful.

Gabe tugged the ottoman away from the coffee table, putting a little extra distance between them, and sat. The footstool was a little short for his long legs, pushing his knees up close to his chest. Alicia's lips curved but she managed not to laugh at what Gabe was sure must be a comical sight.

"What do you plan to do tomorrow while I'm at work?" she asked him after a few seconds of uncomfortable silence.

"I'm hoping you'll leave me the files on the other murder cases to look through," he answered, although that was only part of what he had planned for tomorrow.

He also intended to do a little snooping around Tony Evans and see if anything worrisome turned up, but Alicia didn't have to know about that little plan.

"I can do that," she agreed. "I won't have time to do any work on my dissertation between classes tomorrow, anyway. Marlon and I are planning to do a lab inventory on Saturday to see what items need restocking, so I'm going to try to do a little preliminary organizing between classes tomorrow in preparation." She grimaced. "Does that make me sound like a nerd?"

He grinned. "A little. But nerd looks cute on you."

She frowned. "Gabe—"

"I promised not to try to seduce you. I never said I wouldn't flirt."

The corners of her lips twitched. "On that note, I think it's time to turn in. Do you have everything you need out here? Blankets, pillows?"

Everything but you, he thought. "Yeah, I'm fine."

She walked to the hall, pausing in the doorway to look back at him. "This is going to be an interesting few days."

As she turned and disappeared into the hall, he slumped forward, resting his head in his hands. His whole body seemed to be a live wire, trembling and twitching, just waiting for something to come along and set off sparks.

Interesting few days?

That was the understatement of the year.

Chapter Twelve

Cissy Cooper was in Alicia's first lab of the day. She arrived early and crossed to Alicia's desk, where she was stealing a moment to check for critical updates to the lab's library of software programs.

"So, did you and Unlce Gabe find anything outside last night?" Cissy asked, perching on the edge of the desk.

Alicia finished jotting a note to herself and looked up, struck for the first time how much Cissy looked like her uncle. The Cooper family genes were apparently as overwhelming as the people who possessed them. "No. I was hoping, but I guess I wasn't really surprised."

"It's so creepy, thinking about that guy standing out there, watching you."

"What guy?"

Alicia and Cissy both turned at the sound of Marlon Dyson's voice. Alicia's lab partner stood in the doorway, his sandy eyebrows raised.

Alicia glanced at Cissy. "Nobody, really—just a guy who was staring at me a little too long outside. I think the coed murders have all of us women spooked."

"Very spooked," Cissy admitted. "My uncle thinks I should leave town as soon as I finish my chem final this afternoon."

"He sounds a little overprotective." Marlon crossed to his desk next to Alicia's. "You don't even fit the profile."

"I know. But he just worries." Cissy slid off Alicia's desk and headed to her station near the back of the lab.

Marlon put his briefcase on his desk and crossed to where Alicia sat. Bending toward her, he murmured, "So, really, a guy staring at you spooked you? Who are you and what have you done with the Alicia Solano I know?"

She should have known Marlon would see through her fib. "Okay, fine. Just don't let it get around, okay?" She lowered her voice even more. "Last night, Gabe Cooper spotted someone lurking outside my apartment, watching the place."

Marlon looked surprised. "Did you see him?"

"No, by the time Gabe realized what he was seeing, the guy was already on the move."

"Hmm." There was a note of skepticism in Marlon's voice that surprised her.

"Hmm?"

"Well, weird that this guy just comes to town, conveniently stumbles across a murder like the ones you've been investigating and then happens to see some guy lurking outside your apartment, rendering himself damned near indispensible to you. I bet he's offered to stay at your place to protect you, hasn't he?"

Alicia frowned at Marlon. "I'm glad he's there, actually."

"Well, sure. Thanks to him, you're convinced you're in danger. Again, pretty convenient."

"You think Gabe's setting me up?" Alicia's stomach knotted as she realized Marlon was serious.

"The timing is really strange, don't you think?" Marlon glanced toward the back of the room, where Cissy was already working on the computer at her station. He lowered his voice. "Isn't he the guy who found that other body, all those years ago? And now he finds another body the first night he's here in Millbridge? How do you know he's not one of the guys you've been looking for?"

"Because Victor Logan was one of the two men behind Brenda Cooper's murder," Alicia answered tightly. Of that, she was convinced. "What do you want me to do, ask Gabe to account for his whereabouts for every murder in my files?"

"It would be a start."

Students were filing into the classroom, forcing her to table the discussion. "What do you have after this lab?" she asked Marlon. She had a free period and had planned to stop by the university food court to grab lunch.

"I'm filling in for Doctor Kline next period, then I have an appointment off campus." He gave her a considering look. "I could meet you later if you want to talk."

She'd promised Gabe she'd call as soon as her classes were over. But if there was any chance Marlon could be right, that she'd been duped—

"No," she said aloud, almost before she realized she'd made a decision. "We'll just plan to have lunch tomorrow after labs and we can talk about this more."

"So you're going to let him stay there with you anyway?"

"We'll talk about it tomorrow," she answered firmly, turning her attention to her notes for that day's lab.

But turning her mind from the doubts Marlon's words had raised proved much harder to do.

"YOU'RE DOING WHAT?" Aaron's voice rose a notch over the cell phone.

Gabe shifted his headset and slid a little lower in the front seat of the truck. "I'm tailing a cop."

There was a brief pause on the other end of the line before his brother asked, "Am I going to hate myself for asking why?"

"Probably," Gabe admitted.

"Oh, what the hell? Why?"

"His ex-girlfriend has a stalker and I need to know if it's him or if it's someone who helped kill that convenience store clerk the other night."

"I don't suppose he could be both."

"No, he has an alibi for the other two murders and I'm pretty sure the convenience store murder was connected to the others. But I'm not sure he wasn't the guy I chased outside Alicia's apartment last night." Gabe brought his younger brother up to speed on the investigation, including the detail about the note Alicia had received the day before. "If it's the cop, he might be trying to convince her she needs him back in her life to protect her."

"Which backfired when you stepped in to be her knight in shining armor."

"Something like that." Gabe peered through the windshield. Tony Evans had a first floor unit in a two-story red brick apartment building a few blocks away from the Millbridge Police Department. It hadn't been hard for Gabe to find his place; Alicia's address book had been lying on the kitchen counter in plain sight when he got back to the apartment that morning after following her to work to make sure she arrived safely.

He hadn't really expected to find the police officer at home when he drove by, figuring he'd already be at work. He'd really just come to get a feel for how long it might take Evans to get from home to Alicia's apartment.

But he'd spotted Evans walking to the row of mailboxes at the end of the drive and circled around, parking across the street in front of a dry cleaning business. He saw Evans go inside the apartment. So far, he hadn't come out again.

Aaron released a long-suffering sigh. "Am I going to have to call the Millbridge Police and pull your bacon out of the fire again?"

"Not if I can help it."

"Gabe, be careful." Aaron's tone grew serious. "You know how close Jake and Mariah came to dying last month because of Victor Logan and his rifle-toting buddy. If that's the guy who's stalking Alicia—"

"I know." Gabe had seen the aftermath of the mystery man's handiwork. As ruthless as Victor Logan had been in taking his brother and sister-in-law captive, the man who'd blown up Logan's house had been infinitely more deadly. "Hey, how's the wedding planning going?" Aaron had finally convinced his girlfriend Melissa to marry him.

"We're set for the end of June."

Gabe was surprised. "So soon?"

"Melissa didn't want anything fancy, and now that she's finally said yes, I figured I'd be playing with fire to wait too long. She might change her mind."

"I've seen the way she looks at you, man. She won't be changing her mind."

"Can you believe I'm marrying a lawyer?"

Gabe snorted. "I still haven't gotten used to your being a sheriff's deputy. You're the family delinquent, remember?"

"Keep stalking cops and you may take over the top spot," Aaron warned. Gabe could tell his brother was only half joking.

Gabe spotted Evans coming out of the apartment. The police officer walked to a Jeep Cherokee parked three slots down from his apartment door and climbed inside.

"He's on the move," Gabe told his brother. "Gotta go."

"For God's sake, be careful," Aaron said.

Gabe hung up and cranked the truck, waiting until the Cherokee had pulled out of the apartment parking lot and onto the street, heading south.

Toward Mill Valley University.

Gabe wasn't a surveillance expert, but he knew enough to stay several car lengths back. He kept pace with the Jeep, hoping he was wrong about where the policeman was headed, right up to the moment Evans' Jeep turned down the tree-lined drive toward the Mill Valley University Library. But the Jeep drove right past the library and hung a left, heading toward Atchison Hall, the building that housed the School of Behavioral Science. Gabe had been there just this morning, following Alicia's blue Ford to the faculty parking area near the entrance to make sure she arrived at work safely.

Tony parked the Jeep in one of the visitor slots and got out, moving with singular determination toward the entrance. If he noticed Gabe's truck moving slowly past him, heading for another empty parking slot, he gave no sign. Evans stopped at the top step of the entrance porch, reaching into his back pocket to pull out his cell phone. The tail of his jacket shifted upwards, revealing a holstered Smith & Wesson. Answering the phone, Evans continued into the building.

Gabe cut the truck's engine and headed in pursuit, his pulse pounding like a bass drum in his head.

THE MINUTE TONY WALKED INTO the empty lab, his brown eyes soft with concern, Alicia felt like an idiot for calling him. "I'm sorry—you probably had plans for your day off that didn't include holding my hand."

Tony caught her hand in his, giving her fingers a gentle squeeze. "Nothing I had planned beats lunch with you."

She extricated her hand as soon as she could do so politely. Tony had been more ambivalent about their break up than she had and she didn't want to give him any wrong ideas about why she'd called him. "I feel really stupid about it, now. It's not like I didn't make a couple of calls myself after Gabe showed up practically on my doorstep—"

"There's nothing stupid about taking a few precautions," Tony assured her, gesturing toward her desk. He pulled up the empty chair from Marlon's desk and sat in front of her. "Tell me what raised your suspicions about Cooper."

"That's just it. There's nothing to make me suspect him. It's just—I mean, I met him three days ago. And now he's set up camp in my living room, and it's just not like me to let someone into my life that way, and I don't know what I'm thinking half the time—" She stopped short, realizing she was revealing a lot more about the confusing nature of her relationship with Gabe than she'd intended.

She could tell that Tony read into her words exactly what she'd hoped to hide. For a second, his dark eyes revealed an emotion that might have been dismay, but he recovered quickly. "I've never doubted your good judgment and you didn't go wrong this time, either. I made some calls, like you asked. Cooper is about as squeaky clean as you can get. Comes from a good family, several family members in law enforcement, has a good reputation at the sheriff's department where he volunteers—hell, I'd probably hire him to watch my kids, if I had any."

"You couldn't afford me."

Alicia's whole body zinged with surprise at the sound of Gabe's voice. He stood in the lab doorway, arms folded over his chest, his expression humorless and brooding. She didn't know how much of her conversation with Tony he'd overheard, but clearly it had been enough to put him in a black mood.

Tony turned to face Gabe. "Sorry, Cooper. Nothing personal. Doesn't hurt to be thorough."

"No, I get that." Gabe pushed away from the door and closed in, his gaze settling on Alicia. "What I don't get is why you didn't just tell me you were going to check up on me. Why call Evans behind my back?"

Before Alicia could answer, Tony stepped between them. "What are you doing here anyway, Cooper?"

"Following you," Gabe answered flatly.

Alicia went from embarrassed to outraged in the course of a second. "Following Tony?"

Tony laughed. "You suspect me of being Alicia's stalker?"

Gabe shrugged. "Ex-boyfriend who maybe didn't take the breakup quite as well as she did. A cop who'd know all about covert surveillance—gotta admit, if you were in my position, you'd take a look at you, too."

Alicia's cheeks burned. "Gabe, damn it, we talked about this and you agreed—"

"I didn't agree to anything," he said. "In fact, I remember telling you not to get too complacent about trusting anyone until you'd checked things out." He shot a look at Tony. "I guess maybe you took that to heart, huh?"

"Maybe I should have told you I was checking up on you." She narrowed her gaze, giving in to a little flash of anger. "But you should have told me you were going to follow Tony around town today. I'd have given you his address and then you wouldn't have had to sneak into my address book for it."

Gabe flushed a little and she knew her guess had been spot-on. She made a note to keep her address book in a safer place from here on.

"Where did you think I'd lead you?" Tony asked Gabe.

"I wasn't sure. I don't even know if I really think you're

a stalker. I just know you're one of the first guys the cops would look at if we'd called them."

Tony was silent for a moment, as if considering Gabe's words. After a moment, he gave a nod. "I was at a high school awards ceremony when Alicia called last night. My cousin Phil's boy David is on the Class 2 championship baseball team and they got their trophies at the high school. I went along because I was one of David's first baseball coaches. Dozens of people saw me there—and more than a few of them gave me dirty looks when my cell phone rang in the middle of the program and I had to step over them to leave."

Alicia looked at Gabe. He wore a contemplative look, as if he were carefully considering Tony's story. After a beat, his gaze shifted and met hers. "Okay," he said aloud. "He's not the stalker."

"And ignoring the fact that you trailed me all the way here from my apartment, I don't think you're the stalker either," Tony conceded.

Alicia was surprised by just how relieved she felt to hear them both admit what she'd felt certain of all along. "Maybe now we can work together instead of against each other?"

Both men looked at each other, the testosterone back in full force. But at least they weren't at each other's throats. Gabe finally put out his hand and Tony shook it.

"I was about to take Alicia to lunch in the food court on the quad. You're welcome to join us," Tony offered.

"The food here is pretty good." To her chagrin, she sounded embarrassingly eager. *Obvious much, Solano?*

"Tempting an offer as that is, I need to be going over your case notes." He slanted a look toward Tony. "I got a little sidetracked this morning. But I'll walk y'all out."

"What are you looking for?" Tony asked as he walked

with Gabe and Alicia to the exit door. "In the case notes, I mean."

"I just want to go over everything, see if there's some connection between cases Alicia hasn't made yet."

"Gabe has been looking into these murders longer than I have," Alicia told Tony when they reached the front door of Atchison Hall. Gabe opened the door and held it for her. Alicia bit back a grin, thinking how offended her mother would probably be by Gabe's courtly gesture.

Alicia enjoyed the courtliness, herself.

"Because of your sister-in-law?" Tony asked.

"You know about that, huh?" Gabe glanced at Alicia, making her blush again. She'd told Tony everything about the cases, of course, when she asked for his help. She hadn't really considered whether Gabe might have preferred her to be more discreet about his role in the story.

"Just the basics—you found her body. Your family's been conducting its own investigation."

"We've hit a lot of dead ends. I'm hoping this case doesn't turn out to be another one."

"It's not," Alicia said firmly. "The alpha, at least, is the same guy who killed Brenda. I know it."

The three of them paused at the sidewalk. Gabe's truck was down the lot to the left, while the quad and the food court in the student center was to the right. It was time to part ways.

Alicia felt Gabe's gaze on her, and though she tried to ignore it, she couldn't keep her eyes from lifting to meet his. "Call me when you're through with your last class and I'll come here to see you home," he said, his tone intimate. She felt her knees go weak.

Tony shifted at her side, as if he wanted to speak, but he remained quiet. Alicia felt an odd lifting sensation, as if something that had been sitting between her shoulder blades for weeks had finally fallen away. "Okay. I'll call."

Gabe lifted his hand, holding her gaze another second, then turned and headed for his truck. Tony's hand rested briefly on her arm, nudging her to join him walking in the opposite direction. But the moment she turned, his hand dropped away.

"Cooper seems like a good guy," Tony said as they walked together toward the quad. "You may not think you need someone watching your back, but you do. It's not weakness to need someone else, you know."

"I know." She sounded more defensive than she'd intended.

"I'm not sure you do." Tony stopped in front of the library steps, turning to look at her. His expression was uncharacteristically serious. "Look, I know you and I would never work. I love you like gravy biscuits and I know you love me, too, but it's not the kind of love you build a life on."

He was right. It wasn't. It had been exciting and fun, at first, but it had never really felt real.

"But you're never going to find that kind of love if you insist on being so damned alone."

Tears burned behind her eyes, catching her by surprise. "I'm not alone—"

"Yes, you are. Everything you do, you do by yourself. You think anything less is a sign of weakness. That's why I'm actually glad you're letting Cooper play bodyguard for you." He shot her a wry look. "It's a step."

They walked in silence the rest of the way to the student center, speaking again only when they reached the food court and had to decide which micro-restaurant to visit.

Opting for Mexican, they shared a plate of nachos and talked about everything but murder while they ate. Only when they were carrying their trash to the bins near the food court entrance did Alicia bring up the topic again.

"The deeper I go in this case, the more I realize how dangerous these people really are." She led him out into the sunshine. It felt deliciously warm after the overly refrigerated air inside the student center. "Tony, you have to make the detectives investigating the latest murders understand it's not just some creep who likes coeds. These guys have been killing for a while—at least the alpha has."

Tony frowned at her use of the word "alpha." She knew why; the locals preferred to deal in evidence and testimony, not psychological theories. And they certainly weren't going to listen to a twenty-five-year-old female professor from San Francisco whose parents had been police-taunting hippies and whose brother was a terrorist. "I've tried. But I don't have much pull."

"More women are going to get killed. Maybe a lot more."

Maybe me, she added silently.

Tony's expression softened. "I'll try again." He laid his hand on her shoulder. "Meanwhile, let's get you back to class. Do you want me to hang around until it's time to call Cooper?"

"No, of course not. You go enjoy what's left of your day off. I'm fine here." She wasn't lying. She felt safe enough here on campus, surrounded by students, professors and other staffers. This wasn't the kind of place or situation the killers preferred.

The note the beta had left on her doorstep was a threat, one she took seriously.

But he'd have to catch her alone and vulnerable first.

By two, GABE HAD FILLED ten pages of the legal pad he'd found in Alicia's desk drawer. He'd taken the notes partly to familiarize himself with the cases but mostly to compare the victims, to see where their lives intersected.

He ended up dividing them into two groups—the murders that happened while Victor Logan was still in play and the murders that happened afterwards.

Alicia's theory—with which he concurred—was that Victor had been the procurer, the one who'd taken the alpha killer's preferred victim profile and found the right woman in the right circumstances who'd fit the killer's requirements. If so, there should be something connecting all of the victims he procured, something that would have given him access to them, the opportunity to scout out their situations and choose the right time and place to strike.

With Brenda, the obvious connection was the trucking company where she'd worked. Victor Logan had been a mechanic, and Gabe's brother J.D. had recently confirmed that Victor had done some work on the Belmont Trucking Company fleet.

Alicia had flagged eight other murders that happened before Victor Logan's incarceration that fit the victim profile and the killer's signature. She'd done an admirable amount of legwork, checking with the victims' families and former employers. She'd managed to confirm that six of the eight had direct contact with Victor Logan.

For the other two murders, she'd been unable to tie Logan directly to the women, but they'd both worked for businesses that Logan might have reason to frequent. One had been an assistant manager at an auto parts store, while the other had been the manager of an all-night diner about a block from where Logan had lived at the time of the murder.

Gabe rubbed his eyes. How had Alicia compiled so much information in such a short time? He and his family had been looking into Brenda's murder for over a decade, with far less success. Of course, they hadn't been looking for two murderers.

A knock on the door set his nerves on edge. He scooped the files into the desk drawer and locked it with the key Alicia had given him, then crossed to the front door and checked the security peephole.

His brother J.D.'s face filled the fish-eye lens.

Gabe pulled back, surprised. What was J.D. doing here?

He unlocked the door and pulled it open. J.D.'s grim expression made Gabe's stomach ache.

J.D. loomed in the doorway, filling it completely with his massive frame. Rising to his full, intimidating six-foot-four, he spoke in a slow, deadly drawl. "So, Gabe, when were you going to tell me my daughter was living in the same town as a serial killer?"

Chapter Thirteen

Alex's mid afternoon call caught Karl by surprise. He had to excuse himself from a group of people and disappear into an empty stairwell to speak freely. "I didn't expect to hear from you so soon." Alex took great care to keep time and distance between his kills, trying to avoid a pattern that the police might be able to predict.

"I went by Stiller's Food and Fuel a few minutes ago. It's still not open. I imagine the owner quite rues the day he hired Ms. Phelps as a clerk. He's losing business." Alex's accent was cultured and soft, making Karl wonder yet again what his real history might be.

Alex looked like an average, middle-class man in his early forties—polo shirt and khaki trousers when an occasion called for casual wear, or a simple shirt and tie, off-the-rack suits and moderately-priced shoes when he had reason to dress up. But there was a sort of imperial aura about him, a sense that Alex was used to always getting his way, that had convinced Karl that the man's endless supply of money came from old family money rather than some lucky turn at one of the Creek Indian casinos south of Millbridge.

Karl never asked questions, however. He didn't want to end the flow of cash that enabled him to go places and do things he'd never have the chance to do otherwise.

"Why did you go back there?" he asked aloud.

"When did you take up tagging as an artistic outlet?"

Karl sighed. Of course Alex would notice the spray painting on the wall. "I thought the moment should be memorialized." It was a lie, but Karl wasn't about to tell Alex the truth. Alex didn't like his partners to take on their own side projects. A side project had ended Alex's partnership with Victor Logan, after all.

But Karl was smarter than Victor.

"I'm not the Unabomber. I don't need the press or the police to validate my existence." Alex's tone grew hard and cold. "Don't let it happen again."

"I won't," Karl promised. His plans for Alicia would be over soon. Alex need never know about them.

"Good." Alex loved getting his own way. "I trust we won't have to have this conversation again?"

"No, we won't."

Alex hung up without another word. Karl pocketed his phone and left the stairwell, returning to the classroom he'd left when Alex called. Class had not yet convened, so his absence had garnered no attention.

He paused briefly on his way to the classroom, glancing through the narrow glass inset in the psychology laboratory door. He backtracked until he was able to see the instructor's desk. Alicia Solano was sitting behind her desk, her gaze angled downward at something she was reading. Her hair tumbled forward onto her shoulders, as dark as midnight.

Soon, he thought. *Very soon.*

He continued down the hallway toward the classroom, feeling strangely energized.

"How did you find me?" Gabe locked the door behind him and followed J.D. into the center of Alicia's small living room, trying to read his brother's body language. These days, unfortunately, J.D. rarely vacillated much between grim and grimmer. It had been a long time since Gabe had seen his oldest brother smile and mean it.

J.D. turned to face Gabe. "Aaron told me."

"It's barely been three hours since I talked to him."

J.D. shrugged. "Only takes two and a half hours to drive here from home. If you're motivated. Don't suppose you know where Cissy is."

"Taking her last final of the semester."

J.D. nodded, as if Gabe had told him what he wanted to hear. "Aaron's pulling some strings to find her an internship closer to home. I don't want her here this summer."

Gabe agreed, but he'd also seen the fiery determination in his niece's eyes. "Good luck with that."

J.D.'s eyes narrowed. "You think she'll balk?"

"Oh, I know she will. I tried to talk her into packing up last night so she could head home straight from class. She wouldn't hear of it."

J.D. made a growling noise low in his throat. "Stubborn as a pissed off mule. Got that from her mama."

Gabe bit back a snort. If there was a more stubborn cuss on earth than J.D. Cooper, Gabe had yet to meet him. "You hungry? I was thinking about making myself some lunch."

J.D. looked around the apartment. "So, you just moved in with this girl? What do you know about her?"

Gabe couldn't rein in a smile. "Her parents are former radicals who are still pretty out there and her brother was a terrorist who blew himself up. But *she* seems nice enough."

J.D. shot him a black look. "And she lives down the hall from Cissy?"

"Down the porch, whatever." Gabe's grin spread. "Relax, J.D. She's good people. Smart as a whip, good instincts. You'd like her."

"Well, I'm not planning on sticking around long enough to find out." J.D.'s grim expression hardened even more.

"You won't get far pushing Cissy to do something she's determined not to do," Gabe warned.

"She's my kid. I know how to deal with her."

Gabe doubted that. J.D. loved his kids more than his life, but his grief had put a wall between him and his children. Gabe's parents had raised the kids, while J.D. finished out his obligation to the Navy and then spent as much of his spare time as possible following dead-end leads in his wife's murder.

Gabe knew. He'd spent the last twelve years watching it happen, painfully aware of his own responsibility for the unfolding tragedy.

"I think her final was at eleven, so she's probably through by now. You might try her cell phone," he suggested aloud.

"I did, just before I got here. Goes straight to voice mail." J.D. slanted a narrow-eyed look at Gabe. "Aaron didn't tell me much about why you're here. So, why are you here?"

Well, that answered one question Gabe had been pondering—why his brother hadn't immediately insisted on hearing all the details of Alicia's research. Clearly Aaron had limited his tattling to the part about a serial killer on the loose in Millbridge, editing the part about the probable connection to Brenda's murder.

"I stumbled onto a body," he answered.

J.D.'s gaze whipped up to meet Gabe's. Gabe could tell his brother was thinking about that night twelve years ago when he'd found Brenda dead as well.

How often could such a thing happen to the same guy?

"What happened?" J.D. asked, his voice low and taut.

Gabe told J.D. about his fateful stop at the convenience store, leaving out any details J.D. might tie it to Brenda's murder. He knew J.D. would be angry as hell when he found out what Gabe had kept from him, but keeping quiet was worth the risk of his brother's wrath.

Gabe had seen J.D.'s obsession up close, more than once. If his brother sank his teeth into this investigation, and it didn't pan out, this might be the time it finally killed him.

"Anyway, this murder was similar to the others Alicia was trying to profile, so I agreed to help her out, you know, tell her what I could remember." He didn't add the fact that it was Brenda's murder he was telling her about. "And then Alicia got a message that seems to indicate the killer knows who she is and that she's investigating his crimes. She could even be next on his list."

"And she's Cissy's friend?" J.D.'s mind leaped immediately to the same place Gabe's had.

"I told Cissy it wasn't safe to be here. We suspect the guy sending Alicia these notes may know her personally. If he knows Cissy is someone she considers a friend, he may not hesitate to use her as a pawn against Alicia."

"You should have called me."

J.D. was right. Gabe should have told his brother that much, at least. He'd just been so intent on sparing J.D. the potential grief that might come out of this investigation that all he could think about was keeping J.D. as far away from Millbridge and this case as possible. "I'm sorry. You're right. But I *have* been keeping an eye on her."

"You don't know where she is now, do you?" J.D. snapped.

Gabe looked away. "No."

Cold silence pooled between them.

J.D. broke it. "I'm sorry. That was uncalled for." He pulled his phone from the pocket of his jeans and dialed a number. Cissy, no doubt. This time, she answered. "Hey, baby, it's Dad. Where are you?"

Gabe exhaled in relief and sat on the ottoman, listening to his brother's end of the conversation.

"I'm in Millbridge. Thought I'd come by and talk to—" J.D. cut off in midsentence, apparently interrupted. "No, your Uncle Gabe didn't call me." J.D. slanted a look Gabe's way.

Gabe could tell by the growing creases in J.D.'s forehead that Cissy was being just as stubborn with him as she'd been with Gabe the night before. "Look, I'm here. Let's go to dinner and you can catch me up on everything."

Gabe looked away before J.D. saw the alarm in his eyes. Cissy had kept the news of Alicia's investigation into Brenda's murder secret so far, but would she be able to do it face-to-face with her father? Gabe wasn't so sure. He had to talk to Cissy alone for a minute before she headed off anywhere with J.D.

"I'm at your friend's place—" J.D. looked to Gabe, mouthing the word *name*.

"Alicia," Gabe supplied quietly.

"Alicia's place, talking to Gabe. Why don't you meet me here and you can take me to see what you and the girls have done with your place." After a pause, a genuine smile carved lines in J.D.'s craggy face. "I'm sure I've seen messier. I'll see you in a few minutes, baby."

J.D. hung up the phone and looked at Gabe, his smile slowly fading. "She's worried her place is a mess."

"She's a good kid, J.D."

"I know." He sounded defensive.

"Do what you have to do to get her out of here." Gabe's words caught even himself by surprise. He'd meant to argue for patience and respect for his niece's wishes, but the truth was, he was terrified something would happen to her if she stayed in Millbridge any longer. "Guilt might work."

J.D.'s eyes narrowed with suspicion. "What aren't you telling me?"

So much, Gabe thought. "The guy is killing coeds."

"Is there a profile on him yet?"

"That's sort of what Alicia Solano's working on—" A knock on the door gave Gabe the break he needed. After checking through the peephole, he opened the door and let his niece inside Alicia's apartment.

Cissy looked from Gabe to her father, her expression a younger, prettier copy of her father's earlier suspicion. "Did you call Daddy here?" she asked Gabe.

"Nope, not me."

"I found out about the murders. And not from Gabe, so don't look at him like he's peed in your pool," J.D. added when Cissy's gaze whipped up to meet Gabe's. His voice shifted slightly, taking on a tone of censure. "He didn't say a word."

"I suppose you're here to take me back home."

"I'd like to," J.D. admitted.

"And I guess it doesn't matter to you that I've set up an internship here for the summer, huh?"

"It matters to me, of course it does." J.D. took a step toward her, holding out his hand. "Are you going to even give me a proper hello?"

Cissy's angry expression melted into a look of love so fierce it made Gabe's chest hurt. She wrapped her arms around her father's waist and pressed her cheek to his shoulder. "Hey, Daddy. It's so good to see you."

J.D. kissed the top of her head. "Listen, why don't I take you for a snack and we can talk about it, okay? You listen to what I think and I listen to you. How does that sound?"

"Suspiciously like you plan to kidnap me and take me

back to Gossamer Ridge kicking and screaming," Cissy replied, but there was affectionate humor in her voice. "Okay, we'll go out. And you can talk."

J.D. looked over at Gabe. "You want to come, too?"

Gabe shook his head. He suspected Cissy might be more open to persuasion if she didn't feel as if she were being double-teamed. "I've got work to do here."

He saw J.D. and Cissy to the door, watching them through the window until J.D.'s truck pulled onto the street and disappeared from sight. Then he listened to his stomach's growling protests and went to the kitchen to find a snack.

He had just finished eating when another knock on the door detoured him from his beeline back to Alicia's desk for more file perusal. The face on the other side of the peephole caught him by surprise.

He opened the door to find Tony Evans on the other side.

"So," Tony said with a smile, "what do you say we try a little interagency cooperation?"

ALICIA'S LAST CLASS ENDED AT four-thirty, and as she'd promised, she called Gabe for an escort home. He was waiting in the parking lot next to her Ford by the time she gathered her things and walked out to her car.

He rolled down the window, flashing her a smile. "How was your day? After I left, I mean."

"Fine," she answered, although she barely remembered anything about her day after he left, since he'd been invading her thoughts ever since.

Both of her afternoon labs had involved end of semester final exams, leaving her little to do but keep an eye out for signs of cheating. She normally loved test days, as they offered extra time to work on her dissertation research. But today, despite having a pile of new information on the murder cases to ponder, she'd found her mind wandering again and again to Gabe Cooper.

Tony was right. She was tired of being so alone all the time. And it was her own fault.

But figuring a way out of her self-imposed isolation wasn't an easy fix. The issues that drove her to view the world with skeptical cynicism were still there.

Her parents were still academia's version of glitterati, making Alicia's own academic career feel like an endless night in some swanky Hollywood hot spot, where everyone she met wanted to get closer to her because her parents were celebrities. She couldn't trust any friendships formed with eager professors angling for a brush with the greatness of Martin Solano and his glamorous wife Lorraine.

And any attempts to make friends on the other side of the aisle, as she'd come to think of it—the cops, the prosecutors, the forensic scientists who dotted the landscape of her chosen field of study—rarely went past the first mention of her late brother, the terrorist. Only Tony had bothered to see past that part of her life and she knew that even he wasn't comfortable with her parents and their hagiographic view of Sinclair.

So far, neither her parents' reputations nor her brother's crimes had seemed to faze Gabe Cooper, but there was yet another problem where he was concerned: he had his own agenda where these murder cases were concerned. She could make a compelling argument that he saw her mostly as a tool he could use to find the answers he'd been seeking for years. Her usefulness could be what was keeping him around, not her beauty or her charms or her wit. If she was no longer useful to him, how likely was it that Gabe Cooper would still stick around?

Not bloody likely at all, was it?

She parked her Ford in front of the apartment building,

surprised to find Tony's Jeep parked across the street. Tony was waiting for them inside her apartment, seated on the sofa, surrounded by case files and notes.

He barely looked up as they entered, just waved them over. Alicia took a seat next to him on the sofa, while Gabe went into the kitchen and returned with three glasses of sweet tea. He handed a glass to Alicia and set his glass and Tony's on the coffee table in front of them.

"We've been working on this for a couple of hours," Gabe said, waving at a row of yellow lined notebook pages spread out across the coffee table. "At first, we got bogged down in some of the older cases, but we decided they weren't pertinent at the moment, since we're pretty sure a different beta was involved in those, and the key to this whole thing is definitely the beta."

"Because outside of the signature and the M.O., which in all the cases hasn't really changed, most of the variables can be attributed to the beta killer," Tony added. "His personality. His connections. His passions."

Alicia looked from one man to the other, caught off guard by the sheer force of their determination. She hadn't expected them to be anything more than civil to each other and here they were joining forces and working together like they'd been partnered for years. "I agree," she said, although she'd never really separated the cases that way, not in her mind, anyway.

She had been thinking academically, piecing the cases into a narrative she could type up in a doctoral dissertation to earn her degree. She was passionate about the work, but not in the same way Tony and Gabe were. Tony was a cop, whose hunger for justice had led him into uniform and danger. He wanted results, not just profiles and statistics.

And something even more powerful than justice drove Gabe. Call it vengeance, call it a blood debt—Gabe needed a resolution to his family's suffering and loss. He needed results, too, but this case was so much more personal to him than to her or to Tony.

So what if he was just using her to find the truth that had eluded the Coopers for so long? She was a big girl. She could take it. Being part of giving Gabe the closure he needed was worth it to her.

So was bringing justice to a couple of ruthless killers.

"We're down to the women who were killed in the last four years, after Victor Logan went to jail," Gabe said, picking through the sheets of paper until he'd extracted six sheets. "There's a pretty large gap of time between Victor's incarceration date and the next murder we have on record. I suppose it's possible there are murders we don't know about—"

"We know we're missing several, if there are really twenty-one of them," Tony agreed.

"But I think it's likely that most of the missing murders happened during the Victor Logan era," Gabe concluded. "Reporting and forensics have gotten better every year, and more recent murders are probably better documented and easier to find in records searches."

Alicia felt a smile bubbling up, unstoppable. "Look at you guys. Playing nice and getting things done."

"Well, I'm through playing nice for the day," Tony said, rising to his feet. "It's nearly dinnertime, so I should clear out of here—"

"You could stay for dinner," Alicia suggested, not sure she was ready to be left alone with Gabe when he was in such an intense mood. She'd found him hard enough to resist when he was flirty and charming. Add the fire she saw flashing in his eyes and he was downright dangerous.

"Nope. I have plans." Tony smiled down at her. "Got a date with Ellie from the property room."

After the tiniest spark of territorial jealousy, Alicia smiled. Tony was a good guy and she knew Ellie had nursed a big crush on him for a while. They'd have fun together. Maybe more—who knew? "Have a good time. Say hi to Ellie for me."

After Tony left, Gabe slanted a look at Alicia. "You don't usually tell your new main squeeze that your old one says hi."

"Main squeeze?" She rolled her eyes. "You need to update your slang, geezer." She reached for one of the sheets of paper Gabe had laid out on the coffee table.

He reached across and stilled her hand, making her look up at him. "Are you really okay with it?"

She frowned, not following for a moment. Then she realized they were still on the subject of Tony and his date. "Of course. We've been over for months. I'm happy he's moving on."

Gabe held onto her hand a few seconds longer, finally letting go to pick up the paper she'd been reaching for and hand it to her. "You agree that we should focus on the newest murders, right?"

"I do. It's good insight and a better use of our time." She'd been so caught up in tying all the cases together that she'd lost sight of what would work best for solving the case. "Anything jump out at you so far?"

"There's some information missing here and there—for instance, this case in Meridian, Mississippi—" Gabe picked up one of the sheets of handwritten notes. "Kellie Davis. Twenty-six years old. Waitress at an all-night diner where she was murdered. But that diner is only a half mile from Meridian Community College. Could she have been a part-time student? These files don't say, but we should look into it."

"Can I borrow this?" Alicia reached for the notebook

lying on the table next to the spread-out papers. She pulled a pen from her briefcase and jotted a note. "We're going on the premise that the more recent murders are all somehow connected to universities or colleges?"

"Well, we know the most recent three are. And of the other three murders, one of them is a definite yes—Maleah Kramer was a student at the University of West Alabama over in Livingston. I wouldn't be surprised if these other two were also students."

"Which means the more recent beta also has a connection to the universities." Alicia tried to keep her focus cool and professional, but a hot, curling sensation was running through her belly like a mass of snakes.

"That's what I'm thinking." Gabe looked up from his notes. "Since we're talking about at least three different universities in the last four or five years, it's probably a student, don't you think?"

Alicia nodded, but her mind was already racing through the potential numbers. Though a small university by most standards, Mill Valley had around five thousand part-time and full time students. The male-female ratio was two males for every three females, which dropped the number down to two thousand. Age would eliminate some but not all. "How old do we suppose the beta would have to be? Could he have started as early as sixteen or seventeen?"

"Maybe." Gabe shrugged. "There've been some pretty young serial killers, and since there's an older mentor involved, the beta could have been very young when he started."

"Then maybe Tyler Landon could be the killer." She had to swallow the lump in her throat to get the words out.

"Maybe. Maybe not." Gabe moved to sit next to her on the sofa. When he looked up at her, his blue eyes were smoky with desire. "It's not like it's a stretch that a young guy might find you irresistible."

There she went, melting again at the mere sound of his honey-thick drawl. She tried laughing his comment off. "Apparently, I'm quite the stalker magnet."

Gabe didn't laugh with her. "You have no idea how beautiful you are, do you?"

Her flippant reply died in her throat as she turned to find his face inches from hers. Fear battled with desire for control of her body.

Desire won, at least for as long as it took for her to lean forward and meet his descending mouth.

He tasted so good, a combination of the sweet tea he'd just drunk in lieu of lunch and a darker, richer flavor that belonged only to him. She wanted to drink him dry.

Gabe was the one who pulled away this time, leaving her so off balance she had to grab the back of the sofa to keep from falling into his lap. "Wait a minute."

She stared at him, still feeling as if the world had pitched sideways beneath her. "What?"

He turned and scooped up the notes he'd made, scanning them for a couple of seconds before he turned back to her, his expression a battle between triumph and dismay. "Behavioral Science," he said aloud. "All of these women were connected in some way to the Behavioral Science departments at their schools."

Her heart dipped to her stomach. "All of them?"

He caught her arms in his big, strong hands and pulled her to face him, his expression intense. "You can't go back to that college."

Chapter Fourteen

"It's just a few more days and then the semester's done." Alicia's jaw was set in stone. "I'm not working the summer session. I'll go somewhere. Maybe Hawaii." She flashed Gabe a tense grin that he knew was supposed to be flippant and breezy.

She was just too damned terrified to pull it off.

Still, he hadn't been able to change her mind about working out the last week of the semester, despite spending the last half hour outlining every dire possibility he could think of. "You can get that friend of yours—Mark or whatever—"

"Marlon Dyson," she supplied.

"Get Marlon to cover your classes."

"He has some classes at the same time as mine."

"Alicia—"

She caught his hand, stopping his relentless pacing. "You know what we need? Food."

"I'm not hungry."

Her smile was genuine this time, edged with wicked humor. "Food is fuel, Gabe."

Her smile turned his stomach inside out. "Dirty pool, Solano, throwing my words back at me."

She stood up, twining her fingers with his. "There's a place in walking distance from here."

"It's not safe."

"I'll be safe if you're with me," she said firmly. The weight of her trust in his ability to keep her safe was both humbling and terrifying.

He couldn't let her down.

"Okay," he conceded, letting her lead him out of the apartment and down the steps to the sidewalk.

"It's a Lebanese diner—a hole-in-the-wall, really," she told him as they headed for University Drive and walked right, toward the school. "Naji Garnem runs the place—his daughter Eliana was one of my students last semester and she introduced me to the place. Amazing tabouli and the best falafel I've ever had anywhere."

"I thought San Francisco had the best food anywhere." Gabe glanced at their entwined hands. She hadn't let go of his hand when they reached the sidewalk. Fine with him; he liked the feel of her small, soft fingers threaded through his, probably more than he should.

"San Francisco has great food," she agreed, "but here's a little secret. It's not nearly as amazing as its residents like to pretend. No place is."

"Ah, but you've never been to Gossamer Ridge," he said with a smile. "Ten minutes out on the lake with me in my bass boat and you'd never want to go anywhere else."

She darted a look at him. "Is that a come-on?"

It hadn't been, but her teasing mood was contagious. "Is it working?"

Her eyebrows flicked upward and she flashed a pair of dimples at him. "Maybe a little."

"If this is your idea of distracting me from our earlier discussion—"

"Argument," she corrected.

"Discussion," he insisted. "And if you think you'll distract me with food and flirtation, you're…probably right. But not forever."

"I'm actually trying to refocus you onto something that's actually feasible." Alicia pointed toward a small brick building at the corner ahead. "That's the Cedars Café."

The place was tiny and nondescript from the outside, but when they entered the cafe, it was like stepping into another world. Beautiful photos of the Lebanese landscape lined the walls—not professional travel photos, clearly, but images shot with such obvious love for the subject matter that Gabe found himself wishing he could take the next flight to Beirut.

The images were eclipsed only by the spicy aromas permeating every inch of the café—cumin, cinnamon, garlic, thyme and mint were a few that Gabe recognized. At the counter, a glass front case displayed an array of à la carte items such as pistachios, baklava triangles, fresh-baked pita bread and small containers of creamy hummus.

Alicia ordered an appetizer sampler that included hummus, grilled lamb and something called kibbe, which Alicia explained was a sort of spicy meatball made with ground beef and bulgur wheat. They also ordered falafel wraps, which Alicia didn't have to explain to him, because the crunchy chickpea patties were among Gabe's favorite foods.

"There's a place in Birmingham that has amazing falafel wraps," he told Alicia later, as they ate outside at one of the two tiny bistro tables that served as the Cedars Café's outdoor dining area. The other table was currently unoccupied, though Gabe wasn't sure how long it would remain that way, since the crowd inside the diner had been larger than he'd expected.

"Well, you'll have to take me there before we head for Gossamer Ridge, since I'd like to try those falafel wraps before I embark on my slavish devotion to your bass boat."

"I like to think of the devotion as less slavish and more passionate."

She grinned. "Yeah, I bet you like to think that."

As tempting as it was to sit here and flirt away the evening with Alicia in her devilish mood, he couldn't let her distract him from the danger that encroached like the coming night, muting the vivid colors and warm light of the waning afternoon. He laid down his half-eaten falafel wrap and waited until she looked up at him to speak. "I still think you need to get out of town for a while."

"For how long? Until somebody catches the killers? What if that doesn't happen for months? Or years?" She laid her wrap on the plate in front of her as well, dropping the pretense that her only worry was whether or not there'd be any baklava left if she wanted dessert later. "I can't let these men control my life that way. If they're so intent on killing me, maybe we should just let them try."

He grabbed her hand, his grip tighter than he intended. He loosened his fingers when she winced. "Don't even joke about that, Alicia. You're not going to play bait."

"I'm not planning to," she said firmly. "But I also don't plan to give them any opportunities to catch me alone. I'm going to take precautions. You can follow me to and from the university, or I can get Tony or Marlon to do it."

"Wait a minute. How do we know the killer isn't Marlon?" Gabe asked. "I mean, we think he's someone connected to the Behavioral Science department, and Marlon's the right age. He's in good shape, so he could even be the guy who killed Victor Logan."

"Marlon can't be *that* guy," Alicia disagreed. "Victor Logan was murdered during Mill Valley's spring break and

Marlon spent that week with his parents on a trip to France, Italy and Germany. I've seen the trip photos."

"Okay, probably not Marlon then," Gabe conceded, "but is he really going to be able to fight off a couple of killers if they decide to make a bold move?"

"Can you?"

"Damned straight I can," he answered, and realized he meant it. He may have failed miserably at protecting Brenda twelve years ago, but he wasn't that same, careless kid anymore, was he? He'd learned a lot of things about life and responsibility over the intervening years, much of it self-taught as a direct response to his earlier failure.

"You sound so sure," she murmured, turning her palm over until it met his, reminding him that he was still holding her hand. "You've talked about protecting me before, but there's always been a little hesitation. But not now."

He held her gaze. "If anyone tries to hurt you on my watch, I'll kill them if necessary."

No doubts. No hesitation.

She looked troubled by his words, but also relieved. "I hope it never comes to that."

"I hope not, either."

She took a long, shaky breath, sliding her hand away from his. "Okay, it's not Marlon and we agree it's not Tony."

"That kid who hit on you is a real possibility." Gabe's neck hair prickled at the thought of that teenage punk's attitude toward Alicia just because she didn't respond to his advances the way he hoped. "The way he behaved is pretty aggressive."

"Maybe." Alicia didn't look convinced. "I can't help thinking it was too aggressive, really. Neither the alpha killer nor the beta seems driven by impulse. They're organized. Careful. I'm betting they both have a lot of practice keeping their real selves hidden. Tyler Landon wasn't nearly that controlled. I just don't think he fits the profile."

"Profiles have been wrong before."

She gave him an odd look, as if his words had hurt her. "Of course. I just don't think I'm wrong about this."

"I still think Tony's right to give him a good, hard look."

"I agree with that."

"What about other people? Anyone else at the college strike you as strange?"

She reached into her purse and pulled out a small notebook. She wrote down Tyler Landon's name and added a small question mark next to it. "There's an adjunct professor in the sociology department—Terence Lowell—who's always staring at the female students. It's apparently creepy enough that a few of them have mentioned his attention to me."

"Do you know him?"

"We've met a few times at faculty events. He seems okay, at least with the teachers."

"Present company excepted, I'm guessing most of the teachers don't look much like twenty-year-old coeds." A dark thought suddenly occurred to him. "Was Cissy one of the students who came to you about this Lowell guy?"

"Down, boy. Challenging people to duels is still illegal in this state," she said with a smile. "As far as I know, Cissy's never had any classes with him." She cocked her head. "You're so protective of her. Does it have anything to do with finding her mother dead?"

Gabe looked down at his half-eaten dinner, his appetite crumbling, corroded by guilt. "It has everything to do with it," he admitted. "It was my fault."

Her eyes narrowed with confusion. "Because you found her?"

"Because I failed her."

She shook her head. "I don't get it—"

"I was supposed to meet her before her shift was over at the trucking company where she worked. It was a late night shift—three-to-eleven. Her car had been acting up and she was afraid the battery would be dead when she left work, so she asked me to meet her there at the end of her shift in case she needed her battery jumped or a ride or something."

Alicia's expression shifted from confusion to sadness. "You were late."

"It just didn't seem that important, you know? To pay attention to the time. I was twenty-one and fresh out of college, trying to figure out what I was going to do with my life and it so happened that she asked me for this favor the same day a friend of mine was in town for a couple of days, a quick stop between college and his new job."

"Why didn't she call someone else, like her husband?"

"J.D. was still in the Navy. He was on an assignment. My other brothers were spread out all over the place—the Marine Corps, college—and my sister was only seventeen at the time. She was helping my parents watch Cissy and her brother Michael."

"So it was up to you."

"I meant to be on time. I didn't drink much of anything at the pool hall, just one beer, because I knew I had to pick up Brenda." He pressed his fingertips to his throbbing temple. "I just lost track of time. One minute everything was fine, the next I looked up at the clock and saw that it was after eleven. I dropped everything and broke about a hundred traffic laws to get to her."

"But it was too late."

"My brother J.D. tries to act like it doesn't matter, like he doesn't think about my failure every day. But I know he does. And I don't know what I'm going to do when Cissy finds out about what I did—"

"I already know."

The sound of his niece's voice sent an electric jolt through him. He twisted in his seat and found his brother and Cissy standing a couple of feet away.

"Dad told me," Cissy said. She looked at Alicia. "Hi, Alicia."

"Hi, Cissy." Rising, Alicia looked past her to J.D. "You must be Cissy's father."

J.D. stepped forward and shook her hand. "J.D. Cooper. Nice to meet you. You're younger than I expected."

Alicia smiled, darting a quick look at Gabe. He smiled and shrugged. J.D. was gruff and blunt. Once you got to know him, it was a big part of his charm, but it could be a little confounding on first meeting. "Nice to meet you, too, Mr. Cooper. Cissy's one of my favorite people."

"Cissy has good things to say about you, too," J.D. said quickly, infusing the words with extra enthusiasm, as if he realized his first stab at a polite greeting had fallen short. Unfortunately, it only came across as trying too hard. To his credit, J.D. seemed to recognize that fact as well, and subsided to his normal growly understatement. "She's got good sense." J.D. glanced at his daughter. "Sooner or later, anyway."

"Which is Dad's way of saying I agreed with him about going home," Cissy said, looking at her father with long-suffering affection.

"Good," Gabe said. "It's the right choice."

"I really just came to say goodbye before I left. I dropped by Alicia's but you weren't there. One of my roommates said she'd seen the two of you walking this way and I had a hunch Alicia might be taking you here to Cedars."

"That predictable, huh?" Alicia smiled sheepishly.

"Now that we're here, I'm kind of hungry." Cissy turned to her father, tucking her arm through his. "How about a lamb gyro for the road, Daddy?"

J.D. made a growly sound low in his throat that could have been frustration or assent. With him, it was hard to know sometimes. But he pulled his wallet out of his pocket.

"You coming?" he asked Cissy when he reached the door and she hadn't budged.

"I just wanted to say goodbye to Alicia. Lamb gyro. Oh, and some baked pita chips."

With another rumbling growl, J.D. went into the café.

"I haven't told him about the connection between these murders and Mom's," Cissy said quickly as soon as he was out of sight. "I don't want him to know. Not yet. In fact, that's really why I agreed to go home. If he stayed here trying to talk me into going with him, he might figure out the connection himself."

"And that would be a bad thing?" Alicia asked.

"He's run around after so many false leads that ended up breaking his heart," Cissy explained. "I just don't want him to go through that this time. Not until we're absolutely sure."

"Not until we can deliver a real answer," Gabe agreed. He looked at Cissy. "I'm sorry, you know. More than I can say. About your mama, I mean."

Cissy laid her hand on his arm. "I know. You've done everything you could over the years to make it up to us. But you didn't kill her. Nobody blames you."

"How long have you known?"

"Dad told me when I turned sixteen."

Three years ago. She'd known that long and never said a thing. And J.D. hadn't seen fit to warn him, either.

Not that he had a right to question when or how his

brother chose to tell his own daughter that her mother was dead because her Uncle Gabe was a self-absorbed loser who couldn't bother to keep track of time one night out of his sorry life.

"What did your dad say?" Gabe hated himself for asking, but J.D. had spent most of the last twelve years trying to avoid talking to Gabe about the night of Brenda's murder. Not a word of blame had ever escaped J.D.'s lips, but Gabe had seen enough recriminations in his brother's eyes to harbor no doubts about his brother's feelings.

"He just told me to think carefully about all the decisions I make in life. You never know when even the most innocent of mistakes will have terrible consequences."

Gabe burned with shame. "A true-life cautionary tale, huh?"

So much about the last few years suddenly made sense.

J.D. emerged from the café, carrying a large paper sack. Cissy said nothing further, just crossed to her father's side. "Don't suppose you bought a bag of that fresh pita bread, did you?"

J.D. reached into the bag and pulled out a small plastic bag of the flat, round bread. "I got some hummus, too," he said with a smile.

"So y'all are heading home?" Gabe crossed to where they stood near the door. "Kiss Mom for me."

"Will do," Cissy said.

J.D.'s smile faded and he looked at Gabe for a long moment, until his silent scrutiny became uncomfortable.

"I don't blame you," he said aloud.

Gabe couldn't tell if he meant it or not. "I *am* sorry."

J.D. looked at him another moment, then lifted his large hand and cupped Gabe's face for a moment. "I'll call when we get home so you know we made it safely."

"Thanks." Gabe watched them turn and go, a painful lump in his throat.

Alicia broke the silence a few seconds later. "I sacked up our leftovers. We might feel hungrier later."

He felt her small hand slip into his. Closing his fingers around hers, he turned and looked at her. She was gazing up at him with luminous brown eyes full of sympathy.

"I wish I'd kept track of the time," he murmured.

She leaned her head against his shoulder. "I know."

Gently tugging his hand, she led him away from the café toward her apartment.

THEY HADN'T SEEN HIM. He hadn't made an effort to hide this time. He had every right to be out and about, and Alicia would have thought nothing of spotting him among the crowd of students and locals taking advantage of the warm, beautiful May afternoon.

They had spoken for a few minutes with Cooper's niece and a tall, older man who looked enough like Cooper to convince Karl that he must be Gabe Cooper's brother. Probably Cissy Cooper's father, if their familiar behavior with each other meant anything. If Karl had to guess, Cooper had convinced his brother to come to Millbridge to take his daughter home to the backwoods town they came from.

With women getting killed in the area, he'd want the girl out of town. The only thing that surprised Karl was that it had taken Cooper so long to pull this move. He'd have done the same thing in Cooper's place, though he'd have done it the day Alicia got the note. It didn't take a genius to figure out that a killer targeting Alicia might think of using Cissy as a pawn.

Karl had counted on that assumption.

He'd never had any intention of using Cissy Cooper to get to Alicia. Sure, the idea was tempting. After all, he wasn't like Alex. He didn't focus on curvy, dark-haired, brown-eyed women in their mid-twenties. Frankly, he could see himself enjoying a little alone time with Cissy Cooper and a few select tools he had hidden in the storage closet in his apartment.

But she didn't present an advantageous target. She lived with three other people, which meant she was rarely alone. She'd be missed quickly, a fact that would make it hard to take enough time with her to make it worth the effort.

Alicia, however, was worth the effort. Whatever it took.

If he told Alex what he planned to do, Alex would order him to abort the plan. So he didn't tell Alex.

It would be over tomorrow. Alex wouldn't know until it was a done deal. What could he do? Fire him?

After tomorrow, if everything went the way he planned, Karl wouldn't need Alex anymore.

SHE WAS FLOATING.

The world beneath her feet had disappeared, but she didn't fall. She felt a soft rush of air against her skin, the sensation of rocking in a cradle of warm strength. She tried to open her eyes but her eyelids felt too heavy to budge.

"Shh," a voice rumbled in her ear. "Go back to sleep."

Gabe, she thought, her lips curving automatically. Gabe was here. He was making her float.

And then she wasn't floating anymore. The bands of strength slid from beneath her and she lay, instead, in a field of soft cotton. It felt comforting and familiar, but she wanted the heat back. The solid steel that had borne her high above the distant ground below.

"Don't," she whispered when she felt the warmth abandon her. She reached out with heavy, sluggish hands, trying to keep him from leaving.

Fingers tangled with hers. "I can't—"

"Stay." She tugged his hands, pulling him into the cottony softness beside her. The heat returned, a solid wall that drew her like a moth to a candle. She buried herself in the heat, the strength, until the world around her faded into sweet nothingness.

Alicia slept, unaware that for Gabe, lying next to her in her bed, sleep was damned near impossible.

Chapter Fifteen

Alicia woke with a start. Fragments of her dream chased her into consciousness—a fiery explosion, a guttural cry. She lifted her fingers to her face and felt hot tears on her cheeks.

She had dreamed about Sinclair again.

Closing her eyes in grief, she rolled onto her back and came up against something warm and solid.

Something that gave a low grunt on contact.

Snapping her eyes open, she saw Gabe Cooper's sharp blue eyes staring back at her.

"What are you doing here?" she blurted.

"Sleeping," he answered.

Traces of memory teased her sleepy brain. They'd been working late into the night, making a list of possible suspects at the university, and she had a vague recollection of floating through the air...

She saw, with a mixture of relief and disappointment, that she was still dressed in the shorts and T-shirt she'd donned after they'd returned home from dinner. Gabe was still in his jeans and polo shirt, though his feet were bare.

Entirely too many clothes altogether.

She rolled toward him, pressing her hand against the center of his chest, where his hammering heart gave lie to his calm demeanor. "I asked you to stay," she murmured, remembering more of the night before. "And you did."

He closed his hand over hers, stilling the slow slide of her fingers up his chest. "Let's not play with fire here."

"Let's do." Overwhelmed by a sense of time running out, she pressed closer, brushing her lips against his jaw. "I want to burn. Don't you want to burn?"

He cradled her face between his hands, his eyes dark with hunger. "We talked about this. We agreed—"

"I changed my mind." She pulled him closer until their lips brushed.

He groaned, deep in his throat. "Alicia—"

She silenced his protest with a kiss. Electricity snapped between them as she wound herself around Gabe, longing to be closer until her body was his body, entangled beyond separation.

He rolled her onto her back, his hips pushing into hers, driving her deep into the mattress. She opened her thighs until her sex cradled his, separated only by inconvenient layers of denim and cotton.

He nuzzled her neck, his bristly beard marking her, setting off sparks along her nerve endings. He twined his fingers with hers and pinned her hands against the pillows, gazing down at her with eyes that had gone as dark as the twilight sky.

"We can't—" His words, spoken in a guttural rasp that rumbled from his chest to hers, seemed a feeble last gasp of protest before giving in to the inevitable.

"Stop fighting it." She wriggled her hips until he uttered a low gasp. "I'm tired of worrying about everything. Can't we be happy for just a little while? Please?"

He went utterly still, as if he'd turned to stone. She could almost feel the warmth seeping from him.

"I don't get to be happy." He let her go suddenly and rolled over to sit up on the edge of the bed, his back to her. "I can't make you happy."

She lay still a moment, her body thrumming with arousal, trying to get her sluggish brain to catch up with the sudden, unwelcome turn of events. Pushing to her knees, she crawled across the bed to where he still sat and pressed her cheek against his shoulder. "You didn't kill Brenda. You'd have done everything you could to protect her if you'd known—"

"I didn't do *everything*. You know that." He pushed to his feet. "I need to take a shower. We're looking for Tyler Landon with Tony today, remember?"

Just like that? He was going to walk out of her bedroom and back to the way things were without another word?

"Gabe, we should talk—"

He stopped in the doorway to look at her. "No, we shouldn't. We're running out of time to keep you safe. No more distractions. Tony said we should get started early, in case Landon's trying to get out of town—"

"Wait—I can't go today," she remembered. "I have inventory at the lab." With all the recent distractions, she'd forgotten all about it.

"On a Saturday?"

"It's the only day we have the lab to ourselves." She tried to ignore the flames still flickering low in her belly. Gabe clearly wasn't ready to let go of his control. She wasn't going to seduce him into doing something they'd both regret.

At least, not yet. Many more nights alone with Gabe Cooper and she might be capable of anything.

"I don't like this—you'll be alone—"

"There are Saturday courses in the building, just not in the lab. Marlon will be doing inventory with me, and there's usually a cleaning crew working on Saturdays. It's not like working alone at a convenience store late at night."

"I could stay with you. Tony can handle looking for Tyler alone," Gabe suggested.

She found the suggestion tempting, but there'd be no way she could get much done with Gabe hovering around, a constant distraction. Or temptation. Whichever.

"Go with Tony. I wouldn't wish inventory on my worst enemy. It's mind-numbing. We don't know how much more time we have before the killer strikes again." She didn't add the obvious—that she didn't know how much more time she had before her stalker made good on his implied threat. "You should be doing something constructive."

He looked ready to argue but finally nodded. "I'll take a quick shower, then I'll fix breakfast for us. My turn to prove I know my way around a kitchen." He flashed her a quick smile and then he was gone, heading down the hall to the bathroom.

Alicia sank to the bed, pushing her hair away from her hot face with trembling hands. She was losing all sense of perspective where Gabe Cooper was concerned. It was way past mere attraction and heading somewhere dangerous.

And exciting.

I don't get to be happy. Gabe's bleak words rang in her head, dampening her mood. Had he been punishing himself this way all these years? How many relationships had died on the razor's edge of his guilt?

She had to find the man who killed Brenda Cooper. Not just for her own sake but for Gabe's as well. He was in just as much danger as she was, though the peril to him was emotional—spiritual, even—rather than physical.

He deserved a life. He deserved to be happy. And if solving Brenda's murder was what it took, then Alicia had no choice but to make it happen.

"IT JUST WON'T GO." Alicia looked up from the passenger seat of her Ford Focus, frustration lining her forehead. "And it's after ten. I'm going to be late meeting Marlon."

"He'll wait." Gabe looked around to make sure they weren't blocking traffic. Midmorning on Saturday, traffic was light as the college town slept off an end-of-term Friday night. As soon as the little car had started sputtering, Alicia had pulled over, not far from the Cedars Café, and flagged Gabe down.

"No, he won't. Marlon hates doing inventory and, if I don't show, he'll bug out on me. I'll be stuck doing inventory all by myself until after midnight. It's happened before." She slammed the heel of her hand against the steering wheel and made a growling noise low in her throat. "Damn it."

"I could take a look at the engine."

"And do what? Magically conjure up a new alternator or whatever it needs?"

Gabe knew her irritation wasn't limited to her uncooperative car. He'd hurt her with his rejection that morning. Even though she understood the demons that drove him, she was angry that he wouldn't set aside the complications of his past and just enjoy the here and now with her.

If only he could.

"I'm sorry." She subsided against the car seat, dropping her hands into her lap and looking up at him with remorse. "I shouldn't snap at you. It's not your fault."

"Look, grab your stuff and I'll take you to the university. You can crack the whip over Marlon and then I'll come back and take a look at the car. Is there a particular garage you go to, if I need to have it towed?"

"Donnelly's Garage on Beaker Street. Here, I have the card in the glove box." She dug in the glove compartment until she emerged with a dog-eared business card. She handed it to Gabe as she got out of her car and locked the doors behind her. She removed her car keys from her key chain and handed them to Gabe, then got into the cab of his truck. "Thanks for doing this. I'm sorry I was such a pain earlier."

Gabe felt a stab of guilt. "You weren't. And I'm sorry, about earlier, too. I'm sorry I can't—"

"It's okay. I really do understand." She shot him a wry smile. "Can't say I'm happy about it, but I understand."

At the university, he pulled up by the front door of Atchison Hall and put the truck in park. "You've got your cell phone with you, right?"

She pulled it from the side pocket of her purse and waggled it at him. "All charged up."

"I'll probably be running around with Tony all day, hunting down Tyler Landon and a few other possibles on the list." Before Alicia had run out of steam the night before, she'd helped Gabe compile a list of several males connected to the Behavioral Sciences program who might fit their general description of the stalker—young, physically fit, between the ages of twenty and thirty.

Gabe and Tony would spend the day tracking them down and attempting to assess whether or not they seemed worth a more formal investigation.

Alicia got out of the truck and turned to look at him through the open door of the cab. "I'll call you when we're through, but it could be late. Maybe even into the evening."

"Call me whenever. I'll be here."

Her eyes narrowed. "For now."

"Now's all I've got," he answered gruffly, hating himself.

"So, that's it, then? You spend a few more days here until, what? We catch the killers? What if we don't? What if they do what they've done before, decide it's time to move on? You just pack your bags and you're gone, just like that?"

"I've never lied, Alicia. I've never said anything different." With horror, he saw tears forming in her dark eyes.

She batted the moisture away, her movement jerky with anger. "Okay, then." Her chin came up, the gesture now so familiar to him that he knew exactly what her voice would sound like when she spoke again. Steel on steel.

He was right.

"I'll call when we're done." She turned and ascended the steps to the door of the building, her steps quick and sure.

He watched her all the way inside the building, until the door closed behind her, a tugging sensation behind his breastbone, as if they were attached to each other.

Maybe it had been the high stakes tension of their situation, the constant togetherness foisted upon them by the circumstances, but whatever had created the fertile ground for their growing attachment, Gabe could no longer pretend it didn't exist. It wasn't just sex. It wasn't fleeting attraction or mere admiration. In a lot of ways, he felt as if they knew more about each other than anyone else in the world. Bone deep.

But there wasn't a damned thing he could do about it. He didn't trust himself enough to throw out all caution and take a chance on getting things right with Alicia long-term. He didn't know how anymore. He'd spent his whole damned life in the "right now," once by choice, then later by necessity.

Forever was just a nebulous concept singers sang about and preachers preached about, but it had no meaning to him. For Gabe, nothing was forever.

Nothing but the pain he'd caused.

He went back to Alicia's car, hoping he'd beat the police there. It wouldn't take long in a town this size for a policeman to come by, see it sitting there abandoned with its blinkers on and see the opportunity for a little parking violation revenue.

The car was still where he'd left it, free of tickets and untouched. He used the keys Alicia had left with him to open the car and unlatch the hood, where he quickly found the problem. The car's serpentine belt had snapped and started shutting down engine functions.

It should be an easy enough repair, assuming there were no other underlying problems. He could fix it himself with time, tools and a new belt, but he had none of the above. He was supposed to meet Tony at ten-thirty.

He pulled out his cell phone and called the number Alicia had given him for the garage. The man who answered said he'd have a wrecker service there in minutes.

He hadn't lied; the wrecker arrived within eight minutes. Within ten more minutes, the little Ford was hooked up and on its way to the garage. Gabe had already given the man on the phone his cell phone number if there were any questions, so he headed straight to Tony's place after the wrecker drove away.

Tony met him outside. "Let's take the Jeep. I know my way around town better than you do."

Gabe suspected Tony also wanted to be the one doing the driving just on principle. He let him have the win. After all, Gabe was the one who'd awakened next to the girl that morning.

His brief moment of secret triumph faded as he remembered the look on Alicia's face when she'd walked into Atchison Hall. He certainly wouldn't be waking up in her bed tomorrow. He'd be lucky if she treated him with anything more than the barest courtesy.

He wasn't sure he deserved even that.

Tony asked about Alicia, dragging Gabe out of his morass of self-pity. Gabe told him about the broken serpentine belt.

"Wow, that's a strange coincidence," Tony commented.

"Isn't that what happened to your brother last month when Victor Logan took him and his wife captive?"

"You mean their car breaking down?"

"I mean the serpentine belt breaking," Tony said. "Or, actually, being cut. At least, that's what the police report said—I requested it for Alicia a couple of weeks ago."

Gabe realized he hadn't learned the details from Jake after they escaped that mess last month. He knew the car had been tampered with, but Jake had never told him specifically how. Gabe had been so glad to have his brother back safe and sound after the ordeal that he hadn't asked a lot of questions about how Victor had taken them captive in the first place. "That is weird," he admitted.

"Still, probably just a coincidence. Those belts wear out all the time—I had to replace one just last year." Tony brought the Jeep to a stop in front of a small four unit apartment complex nestled between a dry cleaning store on the corner and a row of modest but well-maintained residences on the other side. He cut the engine.

"Where are we?" Gabe asked.

"Apartment B is currently rented by a guy named Craig Sandifer. Landon's roommate says he crashes here sometimes, usually after he's tied one on and doesn't want the dorm manager to give him flak for dragging in wasted." Tony got out of the Jeep and joined Gabe at the curb. "I figure striking out with Alicia might have put our boy in the mood to drink."

Gabe followed Tony up the sidewalk to Apartment B. Tony pulled a piece of paper from his pocket and showed it to Gabe. It was a black-and-white photocopy of Tyler Landon's Alabama driver's license. "I figure if he's been tossing back the Jack, he probably looks about like that right now."

Tony was right. The bleary-eyed man who answered the

door looked remarkably like his driver's license photo, right down to the bloodshot eyes. "Do you have any idea what time it is?"

Tony checked his watch. "Almost eleven. You Tyler Landon?"

Landon's look of irritation shifted quickly to apprehension. "Who's asking?"

"My name is Tony Evans. This is Gabe Cooper. We're friends of one of your college instructors, Alicia Solano."

Apprehension remained, tinged with a liberal dose of guilt. "Aw, man, did she send y'all to beat me up or something?"

Gabe glanced at Tony, wondering if they could get away with roughing the smart-mouthed kid up a little.

"No, she has no idea we're here," Tony answered.

"Look, if this is about trying to make time with her, where's the crime?" Landon shot Tony a sly look. "Come on, you telling me you never wanted to hit that?"

Gabe squelched the urge to plant his fist in the kid's smug face. "See, Tyler, that's the problem here. I don't like the way you're talking about Alicia. And I'm curious what makes you think that's okay."

Landon looked at Gabe as if he'd just now noticed that Tony wasn't alone. His eyes widened a little, making Gabe wonder if he looked as ferocious as he felt at the moment.

"How long have you been interested in Alicia Solano?" Tony edged between Gabe and Landon.

"Interested in?" Landon's eyes narrowed. "Look, if I'd have known this was going to be such a big deal, I'd have looked elsewhere. There are hot girls all over this town. They're just a little young, you know? Inexperienced. And he said she liked younger guys."

Gabe stepped closer. "He? Who's he?"

Landon squinted as if the midmorning sun was playing

havoc with his brain. "That guy at the school. Hell, I don't know his name. I don't have any classes with him, but he works in the lab with Alicia—Ms. Solano," he corrected quickly as Gabe shifted forward before he could catch himself.

"Marlon Dyson?" Gabe asked, his gut roiling. "About your height, maybe ten pounds heavier, dark blond hair and green eyes? Mid- to late-twenties?"

"Yeah, sounds right." Landon looked suspicious. "Why? You think he was punking me?"

"I'd say so," Tony answered in a wry tone.

Tony asked a few more questions of Landon, but Gabe's mind was already moving in a different direction. Why would Dyson tell this idiot that Alicia might be open to his advances? Was it a joke gone wrong? It made no sense.

All Gabe knew was that he was suddenly very uneasy about Alicia doing inventory alone with her lab partner this morning.

Tyler Landon ended up providing Tony an alibi for the day Alicia received the cryptic note as well as the night Gabe spotted a lurker outside her apartment.

"I'm going to run to the station and see if I can coax one of my detective buddies to give me the go-ahead to look into these alibis on an official basis," Tony said. "You want to come?"

"No, I'd rather go back to the university. I don't like the fact that Marlon Dyson is the one who egged Landon on about hitting on Alicia."

"Sounds more like a bad prank than something serious," Tony said. "And Landon could be lying. Besides, didn't you tell me Alicia said she'd seen pictures proving Marlon couldn't be the guy you're looking for?"

"Yeah," Gabe admitted. "But I'm still going to the university."

Because pictures could be manipulated. And they were already crawling pretty far out on a speculative limb with this investigation as it was. They assumed the guy who'd killed Victor in Mississippi was the new beta killer in the serial killer pair they were hunting, but that was little more than a guess. For all they knew, Victor may have pissed off the wrong people while he was in jail, and the guy who blew up his house could have been a hired gun.

Marlon could still be one of the killers.

He tried to reach Alicia on her cell phone. It went straight to voice mail, so he left a message. "It's Gabe. I'm coming there. Don't go anywhere with anyone."

Tony slanted a look at him. "That'll make her feel completely at ease."

"I'm not sure I want her feeling at ease."

Tony dropped Gabe off at his truck. As Gabe slid behind the wheel, his cell phone rang. He grabbed it quickly, thinking it might be Alicia returning his call. But it was the garage.

"Mr. Cooper, this is Abe at the garage. You were right about the serpentine belt, and we can fix that up for you no problem. But I thought you might want to know that the belt didn't just wear down."

"What do you mean?" Gabe asked, suddenly dreading the mechanic's answer.

"It's been cut," Abe said.

"ALICIA, ARE YOU COMING OR not?" Marlon's voice was edged with impatience.

"I've got a message from Gabe—hold on." Alicia hit the key to play the message, leaving it on speaker. Even through the filter of the cell phone, Gabe's voice sounded urgent. "It's Gabe. I'm coming there. Don't go anywhere with anyone."

She stared at the phone for a moment, waiting for the message to continue. Surely he wouldn't leave her a cryptic voice mail like that without further explanation. But the message ended.

Don't go anywhere with anyone? What on earth had happened to put Gabe on edge? She turned to Marlon, as if her lab partner could answer her question.

As it turned out, he could. Just not the way she expected.

"I'm afraid this is moving faster than I planned," Marlon said, not sounding apologetic at all as he blocked the lab door. He sounded smug, and if Alicia's gaze could move as high as his face, she'd probably see a faint smile curving his lips.

But her attention froze on the large black gun Marlon held leveled squarely at her center mass.

Chapter Sixteen

Alicia's expression was delicious. Fear, yes, but also shock. And hurt. She looked hurt by his sudden betrayal. As if he owed her some sort of loyalty.

Stupid, stupid girl.

"This is a sound suppressor." He thrust the Glock toward her. "It'll make noise if I shoot it, but not much. Nobody will think anything of the sound until it's too late. So it's important that you do exactly as I tell you."

"Or what? I won't get hurt?" Fear filled Alicia's eyes, but also defiance. "You're the beta. Aren't you?"

He bristled at her words. "That's such an ignorant term, Ali. So limited in the scope of your thinking."

"So, you don't see yourself as subordinate to him."

"I'm subordinate to no one."

Her chin came up. "I have seniority here at the lab."

God, he hated her. It would be good, once he got her subdued, to show her just how small and contemptible she really was, running around with her little notes and her psycho-babbling theories about alphas and betas.

He gave the Glock a threatening twitch. "Lot of good that does you now, Ali."

"Where are we going?"

"A place I've prepared," he answered, not wanting to show his hand too soon. He'd gone to some trouble to manipulate her into being stranded here, with no car to help her escape and no one around to hear her if she screamed.

"You'll never be able to take me out of here without someone seeing or hearing." She tried to keep her gaze level with his, but her eyes kept flickering down to the Glock.

He chuckled. "Who said I'm taking you out of here?"

Her gaze snapped up to his again.

"There's no one else in the building," he said, still laughing softly. "And there won't be. I locked the doors with keys I took from the cleaning crew manager right after I had him call his crew and tell them there was a suspected gas leak in the building and they shouldn't plan to work here today."

He could see the struggle in her face, her need to stay strong and in control battling with her growing realization that she was powerless to stop him from doing whatever he wanted.

"If Gabe doesn't hear back from me, he'll come here. Locked doors won't stop him. And he knows you're with me. You can't get out of this one. You think those gloves are going to save you?" Alicia waved a contemptuous hand at the latex gloves he'd donned to keep his prints off the Glock. "Gabe's smart. He'll figure it out. He won't stop until he takes you down."

He arched an eyebrow at the certainty in her voice. How could she be so sure of the loyalty of Gabe Cooper when she'd known him for only a few days? Had their relationship progressed further than he realized?

No matter. He had a gun and the advantage of being the one calling the shots. Let Cooper come. "I'll kill him if he tries to interfere. Now or later."

The sudden horror that darkened Alicia's eyes convinced him he had, in fact, underestimated how close she and Cooper had become.

Bloody fantastic.

He was tired of the Cooper family's interference. Last month, Jake Cooper and his trashy little redneck wife had put Karl and Alex in a precarious situation, forcing them to take time out of their current activities to mop up Victor Logan's mess in Mississippi. And now Gabe Cooper posed a complication that could taint his plan to force Alex to see him as an equal rather than a mere aide.

"Is Marlon your real name?"

"Yes," he snapped, burning. It *was* his name, an old-fashioned name, given to him by his old-fashioned mother whose idea of a stable life was bringing home any man who'd buy the beer and put a little food in the fridge now and then.

She'd named him after the actor because he played tough guys who didn't take crap off anyone. She wanted Marlon to grow up tough, too.

Ironic, really.

He'd grown up tough, all right, and his name had at least something to do with it, since every bully on the block had found his name worthy of vicious taunts.

That's why he thought of himself as Karl these days. Not because Alex gave him the name but because he hated his real one.

"Do you know *his* real name?"

Karl looked at her, a ripple of alarm snaking through him. What sort of question was that? Why would she think to ask it?

Because you don't know his real name.

He circled her, his steps not nearly as smooth and controlled as he would have wished. He twitched his gun hand sharply. "Out the door."

"He didn't even tell you his name?" She feigned surprise, but Karl could tell she was just trying to get under his skin. "Does he know yours?"

"Out the door," he repeated, his voice slower and more forceful.

"Of course he does," she said with a hateful smile. "I bet he knows everything about you—"

"Out!" Rage built in his gut and burned in the center of his chest. He forced it down when it started to slither up his gullet. "Now."

She sprang out the door at a run, catching him off guard. He raced after her, catching up about halfway down the corridor. Grabbing her by the hair, he jerked her around to face him. She cried out in pain, the sound rippling through him like a shot of good whiskey, setting his blood on fire.

She grabbed his gun hand, her grip surprisingly strong. He saw her knee coming up just in time to twist his body, protecting his groin. He jerked her to the side, slamming her into the wall. He heard the shattering of glass and her gasp of pain. He realized Alicia's left hand had slammed into the fire alarm box that hung on the wall just outside the lab.

She grabbed her hand, blood sliding between her fingers and dripping onto the floor. She stared up at him, in shock and pain, and another whiskey shot coursed through his veins, leaving him buzzed and disoriented for a second.

The blood. He had to stop the bleeding or she'd leave a trail for Cooper to follow.

He shrugged off the cotton shirt he wore open over his T-shirt, racing forward to catch Alicia as she took advantage of his distraction to make another run for it. He pinned her to the wall, the gun at her throat, growling a profanity at her as he warned her not to move another inch.

He thrust the shirt into her trembling hands. "Wipe up the blood and then wrap it around your cut. I don't want you bleeding all over the floor."

Nostrils flaring, Alicia did as he asked. When the wound

was wrapped, he tucked his hand under her elbow and pushed her toward the stairs at the end of the hall. When they reached the stairs, he saw her glance upward.

He smiled. *Wrong again, sweetheart.*

She uttered a small gasp when he jerked her toward a narrow door set into the wall. She probably thought the unmarked entry led to a maintenance closet. Most people probably did. Karl suspected the architects who planned the building had made the door as nondescript and uninviting as possible, given that half the people who'd walk through the doors of this school would be teenagers, and some of them would be up to no good.

He'd unlocked the door earlier in anticipation of this moment. In fact, he'd arrived earlier than Alicia would ever have suspected, early enough to intercept the head of the cleaning crew in time to keep the rest of the crew from coming in to hamper his plans.

The door opened to a narrow stairwell down to the basement, where the building's inner workings lay hidden from view.

Alicia resisted as he tugged her down the stairs with him. Maybe she could smell the metallic bite of blood below. He jammed the sound suppressor into her ribs. "Go!"

He pushed her forward into the bowels of the basement. She stumbled through the winding labyrinth, more than once falling to her knees on the hard floor. The third time she fell, he grabbed her up by her injured hand, making her cry out. But the cry cut off suddenly and her body went rigid.

She'd seen the maintenance man's body.

Alicia broke free of his grasp, her eyes blazing with fury. "You crazy son of a bitch! This is between you and me. That poor man didn't have anything to do with this!"

He shot her a look of pure contempt. What did she think,

she could appeal to his sense of fairness by pretending the dead man meant anything to her? She didn't know him. She'd probably never given him a second look when she passed him in the hall on the days when the cleaning crew was working there.

He meant no more to her than he meant to Karl.

"Shut up, Alicia. You don't call the shots here."

Her gaze shifted back to the Glock aimed at her chest. "Your boss doesn't use a gun."

She was trying to goad him, he knew, referring to Alex as his boss. He was on to her tricks. He tamped down his anger and kept his voice even. "I don't plan to shoot you."

She didn't flinch, exactly, but he saw the flicker of fear in her eyes. Adrenaline coursed through him, tightening his muscles and clearing confusion from his brain.

Everything came into sharp focus, from the feral wariness in her eyes to the lingering odor of gas from the trick he'd used to lure the cleaning crew leader down to the basement.

He wished Alex were here right now to see him.

Damn it, why aren't you answering the phone?

Gabe shoved the uncooperative cell phone into his pocket and parked carelessly in front of Atchison Hall, not caring if campus security wrote him a ticket.

He'd called Tony on the way but got his voice mail. He was probably on the phone with his office, calling in favors to get the alibi checks on Landon set into motion. Gabe had left a terse message and tried Alicia's phone again, with no luck.

He expected the doors to be unlocked. But they didn't budge. The doors hadn't been locked that morning when Alicia entered. Why were they locked now?

He scanned the campus, looking for any signs of security.

Surely they'd have keys to get into the building. He didn't spot any rent-a-cops, but at the next building over, a young, well-built man in a white jumpsuit was picking up trash from the sidewalk with a claw grabber and putting it into a large trash bag. Gabe hurried over, flagging him down.

"Do you have keys for Atchison Hall?" He pointed to the building he'd just left.

The young man looked startled. "No, I don't—my crew chief has them, but I'm not sure where he is. But you can't go in there—there's a gas leak."

"A gas leak?" Gabe asked, confused.

"That's what Hector said—Hector's the chief. He radioed in around ten, said someone had discovered a gas leak and he was going down to take a look, but we weren't supposed to go over there until they got it taken care of." The man looked over Gabe's shoulder at Atchison Hall. "Come to think of it, I don't believe I've heard anything from him since."

He had to get into that building, Gabe thought, his tension level multiplying. He didn't believe for a second there was a gas leak. Alicia would have called to tell him so.

Instead, she'd called to say she was going to lunch with Marlon. Marlon, who'd told a punk like Tyler Landon that Alicia might respond to his come-ons because she liked younger men. Whose only alibi for Victor Logan's murder were photographs that Alicia had probably given little more than a few cursory glances. And who, now that Gabe thought about it, fit the general description of the man Jake and Mariah had seen in Mississippi as well as the man Gabe had seen lurking outside Alicia's apartment.

Bloody hell.

"I'm going to find a way into that building," Gabe said over his shoulder as he started toward Atchison Hall. "I have reason to believe people are inside and may be in danger. I need you to go find security and get them here as soon as you can."

He pulled out his phone and called Tony, who answered on the second ring. "Get backup here," Gabe barked as he searched the facade of the building for his best point of entry. There were large windows on the ground floor, but they were several feet off the ground with no easy way to reach them.

"Where's Alicia?" Tony asked, fear in his voice.

"I don't know." Gabe circled to the side of Atchison Hall, spotting what he hoped to see—a large air conditioning unit under one of the tall windows. He caught Tony up as he jogged down to the air conditioning unit. "I'm going in."

"Are you armed?"

"Yes."

"Be careful. I'm about eight minutes away and I'll call in backup." Tony hung up.

Gabe searched the ground for a large rock or something he could use to break the window if necessary. He found a stack of bricks around the back of the building where someone had been doing repairs on the masonry. Grabbing a brick, he ran back to the air conditioner and pulled himself up.

The center of the unit felt a little wobbly, but he stayed on the outer edge and it held his weight without problem. He made his way to the window and stretched out, pushing upward in the vain hope that the window might be unlocked. It didn't budge. Nothing to do but break it.

He hurled the brick at the window. It smashed through, leaving a gaping hole.

He shrugged off his shirt and used it to wrap around his arm, protecting his flesh from the sharp glass. Clearing the lower pane, he hauled himself into the classroom.

He'd been in Atchison Hall only once before, when he'd

followed Tony Evans here when he still considered Tony a suspect. That moment seemed a lifetime ago. He wished he'd paid more attention to his surroundings then.

He had landed in an empty classroom that offered no clues to Alicia's whereabouts. Drawing his Colt 9mm from the holster at his waist, he headed into the hall to search for her lab, hoping like hell that all his suspicions and fears were just the fruits of his imagination.

He didn't make it ten feet down the hall before his hopes were dashed. The glass in the emergency fire alarm box lay shattered on the floor of the hall. Gabe drew closer and spotted blood on the jagged pieces still remaining in the box.

His heart dipped precipitously before hurtling wildly, like a thoroughbred out of the gate. He scanned the hall, looking for signs of more blood. He found more blood drops amid the shards of glass, and a spot that looked as if someone had tried to wipe up a larger amount of blood.

He tried to clear his rattled brain, forcing himself to remember his last time here. The lab had been straight down the hall from the entrance, which lay ahead. He headed in that direction and found a room that looked familiar. He spotted Alicia's purse on the desk nearest the wall and found her cell phone still inside.

Come on, Cooper, think.

If it was Marlon who had Alicia—or even if it wasn't—he'd want to get her somewhere less out in the open than the main hall. He couldn't be sure his ploy—calling in the fake gas scare—would be enough to keep people away from Atchison Hall for long. He'd want to secure Alicia somewhere else. Probably still in the building—he could hardly drag her out of here kicking and screaming. An upper floor?

He went back out to the hall and looked for the stairwell.

He spotted it at the end of the hall. Racing down the corridor, he yanked open the door and was already halfway up to the next landing when he realized he'd seen something odd on the floor below. Reversing course, he returned to the main level. It took a second to spot what he'd seen again. It was a dark red blotch on the floor in front of a closet door.

Gabe crouched and touched his finger to the spot. It was wet. He lifted his finger to his nose, smelling the unmistakable odor of fresh blood.

His pulse pounding like thunder in his head, he opened the closet door and discovered it wasn't a closet, at all.

It was the opening to a hidden set of stairs.

ALICIA AVERTED HER EYES FROM the body on the floor. If she kept looking at Hector Alvarado's lifeless body, she'd be paralyzed by the memories of his constant smile and his proud stories of his daughter and son, who were both on track to win academic scholarships to college. Her mind would fill with the sight of his wallet full of photos of his beloved Ana, who'd fallen in love at first sight when she met him on a trip to Mexico when they were both just seventeen.

She couldn't afford the luxury of grief. Not while Marlon Dyson held a gun aimed at her heart.

She cleared her throat, trying to figure out what would keep him talking rather than moving forward with whatever plans he had for her. "Can you at least tell me this—were there really twenty-one murders?"

"Soon to be twenty-two," Marlon said with a dark smile. "And guess what, Ali? All your little note cards and your files didn't stop a single one of them."

She fought to contain the shudder rippling through her body, focusing on the ache in her left hand, where blood still oozed from her cut. It hurt, though not badly, and the bleeding had slowed considerably, meaning the glass hadn't hit any vital veins or arteries. Probably. She wouldn't bleed out.

At least, not from the cut on her hand.

"Your partner committed them all?" She noticed the twitch of his lips when she said "partner." She'd chosen the word deliberately, offering a small concession to his ego to put his mood on a more even keel. She had to keep him talking, run out the clock until Gabe or Tony figured out that something had gone wrong. Gabe was probably suspicious already, since he'd called to tell her not to go anywhere.

Had he learned something about Marlon that made him suddenly suspicious?

"Yes," Marlon answered her earlier question.

"He's older than you."

"Of course." Marlon sounded impatient, but he didn't make a move to end the conversation. She wondered why. The body on the floor provided irrefutable evidence that he didn't have a problem killing another human being. So why did he suddenly seem hesitant about killing her?

"He worked with Victor Logan for a while, right? Victor found the victims for him. What did he do, work from a list of specifications?"

"Something like that. My associate has specific tastes."

"Females, age twenty-five to thirty, long dark hair, dark eyes, curvy figure—"

"I bet that must have freaked you out," Marlon said, his eyes glittering with amusement. "Discovering you fit the profile almost exactly."

Her heart skipped a beat as a new worry occurred to her. "Did you tell him about me? Is he on his way?"

"He doesn't know about you. Not yet."

"Why not?"

Marlon's smile widened. He reached up with his free hand and retrieved something lying atop one of the enormous galvanized air vents that filled the basement room. Only when the light caught the steel blade did Alicia realize he was holding a large hunting knife.

"Because you're mine," Marlon answered.

Chapter Seventeen

Gabe heard voices. Not close enough for him to make out words, but the muted tones were definitely coming from somewhere in the bowels of Atchison Hall's basement.

He eased down the stairs on the balls of his feet, glad he'd put on rubber-soled athletic shoes rather than boots that morning. He reached the concrete floor and halted, listening as he looked around in an attempt to get his bearings.

The stairwell he'd descended was located at the northeastern corner of the building. Though the stairs were open, there'd still been a landing, which put Gabe's back to the eastern wall of the building.

The cell phone in his pocket vibrated. It made almost no noise, but Gabe grabbed it up and checked the text message Tony had left. *2 units outside. Status?*

He froze for a moment, not sure what to do. Every instinct he had was screaming for him to keep the situation as low-key as possible. He didn't know who had Alicia. He couldn't even be positive she was alive anymore. The voices could be coming from the pair of killers she'd been trying to track down. One of the voices sounded female, but like Alicia's warm alto, the voice was low enough to belong to a man with a tenor voice.

But what if his instincts were wrong? What if he was

walking into a trap that would end up getting both of them killed? Maybe he should let the police handle things.

You don't want to face a world where there's no Alicia, a small, determined voice murmured in his head. *What's it going to take to get her out of here alive?*

He punched in the word *hold* and sent the text, then pocketed the phone and started carefully toward the voices.

THE KNIFE WAS ENORMOUS, the blade at least six inches long. Alicia tried not to focus on the weapon, though it was hard to drag her gaze away from the shiny stainless steel.

Keep him talking. If he's talking, he's not stabbing.

And if he wasn't stabbing, she had a chance to change the balance of power. All she needed was a weapon and an opportunity. Once the knife was in his hand, Marlon had tucked the gun in the waistband of his jeans. It would take a second or two to pull it back out, especially with the silencer still attached. He'd lose valuable time, and that might be all she needed to get the drop on him.

She'd been sneaking looks around the basement, hoping to spot something to use as a weapon. It had taken several glances before she realized the shadowy object lying next to a rickety work table was a crowbar. It was about three feet long and looked looked solid. It would pack a wallop. All she had to do was get to him before he got to the gun.

And before he got to her with the knife.

She wasn't sure why he hadn't come at her already. He seemed hesitant, which she found odd, since she knew he'd killed at least one person with his own hands. And if they were right about the man who'd rigged the gas explosion at Victor Logan's house, he'd tried to kill three others as well.

But an explosion and even a gunshot were entirely different acts from taking a knife and gutting someone face-to-face, she realized. Was that what gave him pause?

"You weren't in Europe last month, were you?" she asked aloud, mostly to answer her own curiosity. "You were in Buckley, Mississippi, blowing up Victor Logan's house."

Marlon's lips curved in a faint smile. "He was so easy to manipulate. I think that's when I figured out what I was really good at, you know."

"You stopped him from shooting Jake and Mariah Cooper, but then you tried to kill them yourself." According to Cissy's retelling of the story, Mariah was Victor's captive in the house and Jake had just gone in to rescue her when the man who set the gas to explode entered and set his plan into motion. "Why? Why not let Victor kill them in the first place?"

"Because that's what he wanted," Marlon answered.

So it really was about control, she thought. She and Gabe had been right to speculate that the note to her and the spray painted message on the side of Stiller's Food and Fuel had been a side project for the beta killer from the beginning.

"Did your associate know what you did in Mississippi?" she asked, her gaze sliding back to the knife he held in his right hand. He was gripping it so tightly his knuckles showed white beneath the latex glove, but still he hadn't made a move.

"He's the one who sent me."

"How did you know what was happening there?"

Marlon laughed, sounding almost relaxed for the first time since he'd picked up the knife. "The damned cable news. Alex saw Victor stalking the Coopers on the midday news."

"Alex?"

Marlon went instantly tense. Clearly he hadn't meant to drop his partner's name. "It's not his real name. I don't even know his real name. And you're not going to live to—" He cut off midsentence, his head snapping to the left, as if he'd heard something behind him. His body twisted until he was facing almost completely away from her, giving Alicia the break she'd hoped for.

She darted to her left and grabbed the crowbar. It was heavy, and she hadn't accounted for how useless her injured left hand would be, but she couldn't let weakness stop her.

Marlon must have heard her steps as she ran up behind him, for he whirled around, his free hand groping for the gun in his waistband. His fingers closed around the butt of the gun.

One of the small rebellions Alicia had indulged in as a teenager had been her determination to play high school softball, a game her parents found a little too pedestrian for their tastes. They'd tried to coax her to play soccer instead, but she'd stuck to her guns. She'd been an average fielder but a damned good clutch hitter.

The crowbar was heavier than any bat she'd ever wielded, but her aim was true, even with the handicap of her wounded hand. The crowbar cracked across Marlon's knuckles where they clutched the butt of the gun. A crunching sound echoed through the basement, eclipsed by Marlon's howl of pain.

Simultaneously came a muted blatting sound. Marlon screamed again as a dark red stain bloomed on the thigh of his jeans.

The blow had caused him to discharge the gun.

A SHRIEK OF PAIN ECHOED THROUGH the basement ahead, sending Gabe's heart leaping into his throat. He forgot about stealth and broke into a run, uncertain whether the cry had belonged to Alicia or her captor.

Another sound—a soft popping noise—registered at the

same time, almost taking his feet out from under him. He'd heard that sound before. It was one of the things he'd learned during his stint at the Sheriff's Academy—the distinct sound made by a pistol with a sound suppressor attached to the barrel.

Another cry followed immediately, drowning out the faint reverberations of the gunshot. Gabe regained his balance and hurtled forward through the obstacle course of pipes and machinery until he spotted movement ahead.

Alicia stood over Marlon Dyson's prone body, her hands gripping a rusty crowbar. One hand was wrapped in what looked like a bloody shirt, but the injury didn't appear life-threatening, he saw with relief.

She hadn't spotted Gabe yet, her attention focused on the man at her feet. "Put down the gun, Marlon. If you shoot me, we're both dead. You hit an artery. Probably your femoral. If you don't get help now, you'll bleed out. You'll never make it back to the stairs."

"Maybe it's worth it." Marlon's gun hand looked bruised and swollen, his grip on the Glock not looking too steady. But all it would take would be one flick of his finger on the trigger to send a bullet tearing through her chest.

"Or I could just shoot you now and be done with it," Gabe suggested, surprised by how calm his voice sounded. God knew, his insides were a quivering mass of sheer terror.

Marlon's body twisted and he tried to level the gun at Gabe, but Alicia swung the crowbar in a beautiful arc and knocked the Glock out of Marlon's shattered fingers. The pistol went airborne, a nice looping base hit that landed several yards away and skittered across the cement floor.

Marlon's shriek of agony filled the air. Still, he had the presence of mind to swing his other arm at Alicia as she darted past him, making Gabe's heart skip another couple of beats as he saw the dim light from the overhead bulbs glint off the stainless steel blade of a six-inch hunting knife.

But Alicia sidestepped him easily and threw herself at Gabe, nearly knocking him from his feet.

Gabe tucked her close, his heart galloping with joyous relief at the feel of her soft, sweet curves pressed against his side. He needed to let Tony know it was okay to bring in the backup, but he also needed to keep his Colt aimed at Marlon Dyson, and nothing on God's green earth would have made him let go of Alicia with his other hand.

"My phone's in my right front pocket," he told her. "There are two Millbridge units outside waiting on my word to move. Call Tony and tell them where we are."

As she made the call, Gabe held her more tightly to him, thrilling in the strong, swift beat of her heart against his rib cage and the feel of her arm wrapped firmly against his back.

She was alive. He'd made it in time.

It was only later, when Tony arrived with the cavalry and detectives whisked him and Alicia away for questioning, that Gabe realized the ordeal wasn't really over. Not for his brother J.D. and not for him.

There was still a killer out there. He may have just lost his partner in crime, but he'd already proved he could find a new one when necessary.

But with Marlon in custody, a dangerous wild card, the alpha killer wouldn't hang around Millbridge a second longer than it took to find out that Marlon was under arrest. He'd be gone, to another town, another set of unsuspecting victims. Another twisted soul eager to play his sick games.

Then what? Gabe had never planned to stay here in Millbridge even this long, and with the alpha moving on to greener pastures, the only thing that would be keeping him here sat across town at the Mill Valley University Hospital emergency room, getting her wounded hand stitched up.

And she deserved so much better than him.

ALICIA HADN'T REALLY EXPECTED Gabe to be waiting for her at her apartment when Tony drove her home from the hospital. She'd hoped he'd be there, but after Tony caught her up with everything that had happened since she'd left Atchison Hall, she'd knew there wasn't much to keep him in Millbridge anymore.

Marlon was recovering from surgery to repair the torn artery in his leg. He'd been lucky; when he'd fallen to the floor, the weight of his uninjured leg had applied just enough pressure to the gunshot wound to slow the bleeding, keeping him from losing all his blood volume. The doctors seemed to think he'd live, but he'd lost a lot of blood and they weren't sure whether his brain might be affected. It could be hours, even days, before he was conscious again.

"The story's already all over the local news," Tony had told her grimly. "Dyson's partner will be headed out of town before I get you home."

So it was over. For her, at least. There would be no more coed murders in Millbridge, at least none committed by Marlon Dyson and his partner.

No more reason for Gabe Cooper to stay in town.

But Gabe's truck was parked at the curb when Tony pulled up in front of her apartment.

"Oh, look. Bassmaster Gabe is still here." Tony's wry tone was more teasing than sarcastic. "Guess you were wrong."

"Unless he's just packing his things to leave," she muttered bleakly.

He came around the Jeep and opened her door, helping her out. She was a little woozy from the painkillers the E.R.

doctor had given her after he stitched up her cut. "Maybe not. Maybe you should give him the benefit of the doubt."

But she'd been right. When Tony opened the door for her, Gabe stood in front of the sofa, packing clothes into the soft-sided duffel bag he used as a suitcase.

He looked up, his gaze honing in on her with the intensity of a Klieg light. "Are you sure you're okay? Should you have stayed overnight at the hospital?"

She dropped her gaze to the duffel bag. "The better for you to make a clean getaway?"

He made a low growling noise in his throat. "Look, it's not like that—"

"You know, I think I'm going to go check in at the station, see if there's anything new." Tony backed toward the door.

"No, stay," Alicia said. "This won't take long. I think we said most of what needed to be said this morning."

"Tony, go," Gabe said. "I'll stay with her until you can get back. I promise."

"So you really are going?" Tony sounded disappointed.

"It'll be okay," Gabe insisted.

Alicia wanted to protest, not ready to be left alone with Gabe when he was so obviously about to walk out of her life for good. She'd known this moment was coming—he'd made it clear this morning that he wasn't going to stick around long-term.

She just wasn't ready for that moment to happen now.

But she was a grown woman. She'd taken some hard licks in her life before. She could take this one, too. It would hurt like crazy, but at least she had a heavy-duty dose of pain-killer coursing through her bloodstream. It wouldn't make tomorrow any easier, but maybe it would take the edge off tonight.

Gabe waited until Tony had left the apartment to speak. "I wrote you a note."

"Nice of you." She had meant her words to come out more breezy than bitter, but the drugs were apparently screwing up her grasp of nuance.

"It's pretty much a good-bye," he admitted. "Nice to have met you, have a great life."

"At least you're honest," she muttered, realizing that she even loved his brutal honesty. It was refreshing, if painful as hell. "You want to just read it to me? They gave me the good drugs at the E.R. My eyes are kind of crossing at the moment."

Gabe moved forward, his hands cupping her arms as she started to wobble on her suddenly gelid knees. His touch burned like a brand and she felt all her bravado seeping away.

He helped her to the sofa, shoving his duffel bag onto the floor, where it spilled some of its contents. "Are you okay?"

Her head stopped swimming. "I will be."

He slid his palm up to her jaw, his thumb brushing over her chin and settling on her lower lip. She found it difficult to draw her next breath.

"You deserve a guy who isn't so damaged by his past mistakes. I screwed up so badly and there's no way I can ever fix it." His voice ached. "I was so afraid I was going to be too late today."

She gazed up at him, the world spinning around her as she struggled to focus. "But you weren't. I'm not sure it would have ended as well as it did if you hadn't arrived. I'm pretty sure he meant to kill me, even if he bled to death because of it."

Gabe nodded. "I think you're right."

"You can't punish yourself the rest of your life for one

mistake." The room finally stopped whirling, though clarity wasn't exactly repairing her equilibrium, not with Gabe's sexy lower lip close enough to reach up and nibble. "Nobody expects you to. Not even your brother."

"I know." Gabe bent forward until his forehead touched hers. His breath warmed her cheeks, fragrant with the aroma of coffee and breath mints. "I still have to go."

She closed her eyes, pain tracing a hot arc through her chest. "And that's it? You walk away and never come back?"

"That was the plan," he admitted, pulling his head away. "Right up to the moment you walked through the door."

She opened her eyes. He was gazing at her with a heady mixture of need and desperation. He lifted his other hand, cradling her face between his palms.

"I have to go home. Tonight." Gabe's thumbs caressed her bottom lip. "J.D. doesn't know anything about what's going on—Cissy and I decided not to tell him until we were sure there was a connection. But now we know there is and he needs to hear it from me before he hears it from someone else."

"Tonight?" she repeated bleakly, even though she knew he was right. His brother had to hear the truth from him, as soon as possible.

Gabe's brow creased and she saw a battle going on behind his murky blue eyes. "It'll be all over the news by morning. It has to be tonight. But I don't like the idea of leaving you here alone—do you think Tony—"

"Take me with you," she blurted, catching even herself by surprise. But now that the words were out, the idea seemed bloody brilliant.

"To Gossamer Ridge?"

She nodded. "You don't want to leave me alone. I

don't want you to leave. Taking me with you solves both problems."

He stared at her for a long moment. "I'm not sure I could let you go if you come with me."

She felt a silly grin spreading across her face, no doubt drug-fueled, but she didn't care. "I don't want you to let me go, so that works out."

He released a soft huff of laughter. "You're so high."

"High on love," she said with a giggle that she was pretty sure she'd be mortified to remember in the morning.

"That's just the drugs talking," Gabe said, but he was grinning at her as if she'd just told him he'd won the lottery.

"Probably," she agreed. "So you'd better take advantage of me while I'm stoned, because by morning when I come off this pill, I'm going to be hell on wheels."

"High on love," he repeated, rolling the words around in his mouth as if tasting them. "That does explain it."

She tilted her head back drunkenly to look at him. "Explain what?"

He just grinned at her and dipped his head for a long, world-shattering kiss. When he finally dragged his mouth away from hers, he was laughing. "Stay here, sweetheart. Hold on to this sofa and try to stay off the floor." He backed away from her, sending a flutter of alarm through her belly.

"Where are you going?"

He turned and shot her another self-satisfied grin. "To pack you a bag." He disappeared into her bedroom.

Alicia leaned her head back on the sofa, grinning. In the morning, there'd be a lot to sort out—her job, his guilt, her family—and the leftover loose ends from her ordeal at Atchison Hall. But she knew they'd work things out, one

way or another, for she'd already seen in Gabe's eyes the
same powerful emotion singing in her own veins.

High on love, indeed.

* * * * *

COOPER JUSTICE: COLD CASE INVESTIGATION
comes to a gripping conclusion next month with
COOPER VENGEANCE,
only from Paula Graves—

Look for it wherever
Harlequin Intrigue books are sold!

REQUEST YOUR FREE BOOKS!
2 FREE NOVELS PLUS 2 FREE GIFTS!

❖Harlequin®

INTRIGUE®

BREATHTAKING ROMANTIC SUSPENSE

YES! Please send me 2 FREE Harlequin Intrigue® novels and my 2 FREE gifts (gifts are worth about $10). After receiving them, if I don't wish to receive any more books, I can return the shipping statement marked "cancel." If I don't cancel, I will receive 6 brand-new novels every month and be billed just $4.24 per book in the U.S. or $4.99 per book in Canada. That's a saving of at least 15% off the cover price! It's quite a bargain! Shipping and handling is just 50¢ per book in the U.S. and 75¢ per book in Canada.* I understand that accepting the 2 free books and gifts places me under no obligation to buy anything. I can always return a shipment and cancel at any time. Even if I never buy another book, the two free books and gifts are mine to keep forever.

182/382 HDN FC5H

Name	(PLEASE PRINT)
Address	Apt. #
City	State/Prov.	Zip/Postal Code

Signature (if under 18, a parent or guardian must sign)

Mail to the **Reader Service:**
IN U.S.A.: P.O. Box 1867, Buffalo, NY 14240-1867
IN CANADA: P.O. Box 609, Fort Erie, Ontario L2A 5X3

Not valid for current subscribers to Harlequin Intrigue books.

**Are you a subscriber to Harlequin Intrigue books
and want to receive the larger-print edition?
Call 1-800-873-8635 or visit www.ReaderService.com.**

* Terms and prices subject to change without notice. Prices do not include applicable taxes. Sales tax applicable in N.Y. Canadian residents will be charged applicable taxes. Offer not valid in Quebec. This offer is limited to one order per household. All orders subject to credit approval. Credit or debit balances in a customer's account(s) may be offset by any other outstanding balance owed by or to the customer. Please allow 4 to 6 weeks for delivery. Offer available while quantities last.

Your Privacy—The Reader Service is committed to protecting your privacy. Our Privacy Policy is available online at www.ReaderService.com or upon request from the Reader Service.

We make a portion of our mailing list available to reputable third parties that offer products we believe may interest you. If you prefer that we not exchange your name with third parties, or if you wish to clarify or modify your communication preferences, please visit us at www.ReaderService.com/consumerschoice or write to us at Reader Service Preference Service, P.O. Box 9062, Buffalo, NY 14269. Include your complete name and address.

HI11

Harlequin® Blaze™ brings you
New York Times *and* USA TODAY *bestselling author*
Vicki Lewis Thompson with three new steamy titles
from the bestselling miniseries SONS OF CHANCE

Chance isn't just the last name of these rugged
Wyoming cowboys—it's their motto, too!

Read on for a sneak peek at the first title,
SHOULD'VE BEEN A COWBOY

Available June 2011 only from Harlequin® Blaze™.

"THANKS FOR NOT TURNING ON THE LIGHTS," Tyler said. "I'm a mess."

"Not in my book." Even in low light, Alex had a good view of her yellow shirt plastered to her body. It was all he could do not to reach for her, mud and all. But the next move needed to be hers, not his.

She slicked her wet hair back and squeezed some water out of the ends as she glanced upward. "I like the sound of the rain on a tin roof."

"Me, too."

She met his gaze briefly and looked away. "Where's the sink?"

"At the far end, beyond the last stall."

Tyler's running shoes squished as she walked down the aisle between the rows of stalls. She glanced sideways at Alex. "So how much of a cowboy are you these days? Do you ride the range and stuff?"

"I ride." He liked being able to say that. "Why?"

"Just wondered. Last summer, you were still a city boy. You even told me you weren't the cowboy type, but you're…different now."

He wasn't sure if that was a good thing or a bad thing. Maybe she preferred city boys to cowboys. "How am I different?"

"Well, you dress differently, and your hair's a little longer. Your face seems a little more chiseled, but maybe that's because of your hair. Also, there's something else, something harder to define, an attitude…"

"Are you saying I have an attitude?"

"Not in a bad way. It's more like a quiet confidence."

He was flattered, but still he had to laugh. "I just admitted a while ago that I have all kinds of doubts about this event tomorrow. That doesn't seem like quiet confidence to me."

"This isn't about your job, it's about…your…" She took a deep breath. "It's about your sex appeal, okay? I have no business talking about it, because it will only make me want to do things I shouldn't do." She started toward the end of the barn. "Now, where's that sink? We need to get cleaned up and go back to the house. Dinner is probably ready, and I—"

He spun her around and pulled her into his arms, mud and all. "Let's do those things." Then he kissed her, knowing that she would kiss him back, knowing that this time he would take that kiss where he wanted it to go. And she would let him.

Follow Tyler and Alex's wild adventures in
SHOULD'VE BEEN A COWBOY
Available June 2011 only from Harlequin® Blaze™
wherever books are sold.

❖ Harlequin®

INTRIGUE

USA TODAY BESTSELLING AUTHOR

B.J. DANIELS

**BRINGS READERS THE NEXT
INSTALLMENT IN THE SUSPENSEFUL
MINISERIES**

❧ WHITEHORSE ❧
MONTANA
Chisholm Cattle Company

When Billie Rae Rasmussen literally crashes into
handsome rancher Tanner Chisholm at the local rodeo,
the explosion is bigger than the fair's fireworks.

Tanner quickly realizes this frightened woman
is running from a dark and dangerous secret.

Can he save her?

LASSOED
June 2011

Four more titles to follow....